ABBY VS THE SPLATPLOITATION BROTHERS

HILLBILLY FARM

Abby Vs. The Splatploitation Brothers: Hillbilly Farm
First Edition June 2022
Edited By: Wendy Maynard
Cover Illustration By: JS Adams

ABBY VS THE SPLATPLOITATION BROTHERS

HILLBILLY FARM

STEPHEN COOPER

Splatploitation Press

Hillbilly Farm

A rotten wooden door hung loosely from its framework at the front of a dilapidated farmhouse. The door didn't look fit for purpose to begin with, more like a shed door than a front door, but somehow it had found its way to the big house. Promoted from keeping the tools protected to sheltering whoever, or whatever, waited inside the creepy farmhouse.

Three thin rusted metal bars tried to hold the crumbling wooden planks of the door in place but the whole door gave the impression it would fall apart at any second. The door looked melted too with the way the colour drained by the time it reached the bottom making the house even more uninviting. Speaking of the bottom, the planks didn't come close to touching the ground as they let the warm night air and the light from the impossibly bright moon sneak inside the house with ease. Any rodents, or even a small burglar could easily follow the night into the house with the bottom seemingly ending a foot or two before the door sill. What a fucking useless door. God only knows what state the original must have been in for this to have been considered the better option.

It wasn't just things getting in where the door failed at as a high pitch scream escaped through the many holes in the battered weathered door from inside the house too. An awful stereotypical farmer drawl followed the scream, bellowed from someone who sounded like they could be in their hundreds.

"Get that shaky whore," the vile elderly woman roared in her croaky harsh voice.

Whitney Becker burst through the frail door knocking it further off its hinges. How the fuck it stayed remotely upright was anyone's guess. In her early twenties she looked like a victim straight out of any trashy horror movie. Blonde hair, blue eyes, and cleavage barely staying in her stripy bikini top. Her daisy dukes were soaked in blood. Her long legs caked in mud. To prove her scream teen status she began to run in slow-motion before screaming with all her might, "Somebody help me!"

The girl was obviously petrified. Certainly her scream indicated her terror, and the look in her eyes backed it up. But something didn't seem quite right, like maybe she was acting scared, rather than being scared. Make no mistake this girl really was truly in a terrifying situation, but something was definitely off. As if the tears rolling down her face were a struggle, which they most definitely shouldn't have been.

Her muddy legs couldn't keep up with her body as she sprinted down the farmhouse garden no longer in slow-motion but more full pelt. The tears really were streaming now and her arms were flailing all over the place. Several times on the short run it felt as if she would overbalance and hit the ground hard but each time she somehow managed to stay upright. Whitney had to escape this heinous backwater place.

The garden itself contained an ungodly amount of ruined farming gear. Old pitchforks and spades were dug into the dirt. Wooden barrels, burst tyres, and a broken trough littered the ground. A hose pipe and lawnmower had both long since outlived their warranty. An old swing bench, with missing planks, hung lazily from its broken chains. The grass was long dead and had turned a dirty looking yellow colour All had a very neglected vibe about it, yet clearly some kind of life lived in the house and had terrified the living hell out of poor Whitney.

The house looked like pure evil lived there. Like the farmhouse had grown up aspiring to be the *Texas Chainsaw Massacre* house. No part of it wasn't busted or broken in some way. Every window looked smashed or boarded up. Every plank of wood hung loose covered in rusty nails, or damaged beyond repair. The roof was sliding off, at least that's what seemed to be happening because the angle it was at it should have already hit the ground. How the place still stood was anyone's guess. A strong wind would have effortlessly been able to knock the whole fucking thing over, but fortunately for the house there wasn't any wind… just hysterical screams.

Whitney finally tripped as she reached the end of the long garden landing face first on what remained of the crumbling pavement beneath her. It had been coming from the moment she broke free of the house, but it still surprised her enough not have protected herself. Whitney's forehead bounced off the stony pavement with a sickening thud that almost sounded too loud as she failed to get her hands down in time. A sound that sounded like a cracked skull, or at the very best a concussion. Somehow luckily for Whitney she suffered neither despite head-butting the path. She slowly lifted her head from the ground as bright red blood dripped back down from her forehead, only the blood wasn't hers. Whitney tried to focus on the objects beneath her, although she'd soon wish she hadn't.

Blood was the first thing she saw below her, and lots of it. All different shades of red spewed across the floor washing into each other. Lying amongst the blood were several chunks of flesh and potential body parts. At least that's what it looked like to Whitney during her first blurry glance as she still felt the effects of the harsh pavement. She wanted to be wrong. Wanted her eyes to have deceived her. But unfortunately a lot of what Whitney had hoped was wrong, or had been some kind of trick, turned out to be reality for the poor girl of late.

An abrupt "Oink" interrupted her morbid investigation. Whitney raised her head to see a pig standing alongside her with a human hand sticking from its mouth. Or was it a human hand? It was missing a finger and had most certainly been chewed up by the pig, but the texture of the hand still seemed somehow wrong. Rubbery almost. Whitney watched as several more pigs trotted towards her all with their mouths full. They all carried different body parts that again didn't look quite right in more than the 'that's fucking disgusting why are you carrying a severed hand in your snout' sense.

Just outside the garden fence, beneath the pigs, lay the source of the numerous chewed up body parts… Whitney's friends. A mass of different colour hair, ripped clothes, and limbs littered the pavement. Every available organ was on display within the grotesque pile of former beauties. A loose eye ball stared directly at Whitney, the head it used to belong to sat decapitated slightly further back.

Whitney recognised a formerly rainbow coloured t-shirt amongst the mess that used to belong to her bestie Alice. Now it was all just one dark shade of red, much like Alice herself. She lay about five metres away from Whitney, the former model now looking like she'd been turned inside out, mostly because she had been. One of her legs was hooked over the garden fence while the other was in the snout of another filthy pig staring at Whitney. Fuck knows what happened to her arms, they were long gone. It suddenly dawned on Whitney that it was Alice's head a little further back from the staring eye, which had also belonged to Alice.

She didn't have any screams left in her as she looked down at the mishmash of body parts and organs which used to be her friends and were now an extension of the gore-fest outside. An uncontrollable stream of tears cascaded down Whitney's distraught face while a lump in her throat made it hard for her to even breathe. The word "why" managed to escape quietly from her mouth beneath the sobs. No one was around to hear or answer the question, until a figure emerged from the loose farmhouse door behind her.

The man wore ripped oil-covered dirty overalls and a split straw hat. His skinny underfed frame oozed with ugly boils that looked like they had been painted on. His face appeared both unshaven and shaven at the same time, like he had stopped half way through and completely fucking forgotten he'd started. His rotten teeth alternated between yellow and black with surprising precision, while his nose was hooked like it had been broken and set wrong more than once.

This is who Whitney was running from. A Psycho Hillbilly complete with a rusty pitchfork covered in fresh bloody clumps of human hair and flesh.

"I'm going to feed you to the pigs little girl, Oink, oink oink."

If possible his accent was even worse than his mom's. He stalked towards Whitney smiling at his own shit joke thinking he was king of the fucking world, and in his biased opinion, he was.

He watched as Whitney looked back at him. Her face contorted with fear, frozen fear, the Psycho Hillbilly's favourite kind. He liked it when they just seemed to wait for him to arrive. It wasn't as though he was lazy, he enjoyed a good chase as much as any other fucking crazy deranged psycho slasher killer, but he loved the power of them being so scared they couldn't move. Just frozen to the spot. Waiting for him to kill them in any disgustingly inventive way that he saw fit.

But Whitney wasn't that girl. With one last look at her friends, and an ear-piecing shriek directed at the Psycho Hillbilly, she clambered to her feet in an attempt to escape. It wasn't the best attempt though as she immediately slipped on some loose intestines. Whitney had to use one of the pigs to keep her balance before almost falling over the flimsy garden gate in front of her. She just about managed to stay upright as she swung the gate forward while again slipping on the body parts below her. It would have been farcical in the right comedy setting, but this wasn't a Buster Keaton sketch, and there was nothing funny about her current predicament. Psycho Hillbilly found it funny though as he continued his menacing stalk towards her while laughing at her pathetic attempt to escape him.

Whitney finally rounded the gate still looking as wobbly as fuck - maybe in retrospect she did suffer a concussion after all - before spotting another decapitated head belonging to her friend lying on the floor. She tumbled to the ground beside the formerly pretty head that belonged to Beth. More tears streamed from her terrified eyes. Psycho Hillbilly was just loving it, he couldn't have planned it better.

"That one gave good head," he chuckled in Whitney's direction as he reached her.

He jabbed his pitchfork forward poking Whitney's skinny ass through her blood soaked shorts. Much to his delight she squealed in pain.

"You sound just like the pigs," he bellowed once more. He looked down apologetically at the pigs clearly holding them in much higher regard than the tortured girl in front of him. Before he could come up with another insult Whitney sprang to her feet and dug her fingers into Psycho Hillbilly's face. She scratched hard at his eyes trying to claw them out but it wasn't that easy, especially with all her nails long since broken and barely any energy left in her body. She gave it her best shot though.

Psycho Hillbilly swatted her aside, much less amused than he had been several moments beforehand. The look in his eyes changed from the jovial mean-spirited bastard look he had to something else. Something much more menacing. As if she had crossed some line that he wasn't going to put up with. A look that Whitney recognised would probably spell the end of her if she didn't do something, anything.

But what could she do? Whitney climbed to her feet once

more seemingly spending the last five minutes constantly crawling on the ground and tried to make a run for it. It wasn't a new plan. She'd already used it several times in the last few minutes and failed every time. But really what else could she do?

Psycho Hillbilly's menacing look faded. It turned more into bemusement than the immediate urge to kill. He nodded his approval as Whitney stumbled away once again trying to escape him. He knew she couldn't. There was literally nowhere for her to go. Nowhere for her to run too. Whatever she tried he'd find her, he'd catch her, and he'd fuck her up a little more. That's what always happened. That's what happened to all her friends lying in pieces sprayed out on the pavement before him, and all the young teens that had the unfortunate pleasure of running into him in the past.

This was his land, his farm, his world. He ruled here and they should know fucking better than to cross him, or his mom. He watched as Whitney tried to climb over a barbwire fence, what's left of her clothes snagging on the jagged metal as her exposed skin got further cut up. He'd let her run long enough. Looking down at the filthy pigs circling his feet beneath him he reached down to pick one of them up.

Holding it in his hand he pulled it back like he was ready to hurl it at Whitney…

Abby Jackson

Watching the horror unfold on the 40-inch TV screen in her apartment was Abby Jackson. She sat in her pyjamas on the comfy sofa with a half-filled notepad at her side which she grabbed for when the squeals of a thrown pig echoed from the screen. Abby cringed as she watched the obviously fake pig hit the back of Whitney's head and the Psycho Hillbilly burst into hysterical laughter.

"Everybody loves bacon," he delightfully spat out in his fucking awful southern drawl that somehow sounded a little Irish too.

Even in her pyjama's Abby had hints of a gothic look about her. She wasn't a full blown goth by any means, or a goth in any way in her eyes, but she definitely leaned towards the darker makeup associated with the look. She had shortish raven black hair that hung around the bottom of her face, thickish eye liner, and dark eyebrows that she definitely plucked once in a while but certainly never went overboard with. Her lipstick, when she applied it, tended to also lean towards the darker colours. She had a certain Wednesday Adams vibe about her with her pale skin too but wasn't quite as cold as her. At least that's what she thought. To others it could be somewhat debatable. In fact somewhat didn't quite cover it.

Abby had cultivated this look over a few years and now in her early twenties felt close to perfecting it. She'd try to get that right mix in her eyes of being herself, but also of being a little unapproachable. She fully admitted to being antisocial and awkward, and wanted her look to reflect that. It wasn't designed to scare everyone off per se, more just to limit her social circle and immediate surroundings to people she could tolerate. Maybe it wasn't the best way for Abby to approach life, but there you go.

The apartment was pretty basic despite the large TV and comfy sofa. A coffee table completed the look in the living room, with a few movie posters up on the wall too. Those weren't up there with blue tac and tatty edges though. The three poster on the wall were all framed. *The Shining, Alien,* and *Rear Window* all stood equally spaced apart with thin black fames around each and a clear glass front. All very purposeful. Very elegant. They were regularly polished and maintained more than anything else in the apartment, with one exception.

The pride and joy of the apartment stood on a shelf beside the TV. The shelf contained a bunch of trophies Abby had won for her last short film, '*The Figure in the Woods.*' Best Picture ones. Best Director. Best Editing. There must have been around fifteen all told from a host of different short film festivals across the country. A lot of people will say it's not about the trophies and awards, Abby included when people ask her, but she loved them. It was recognition of going in the right direction. Confirmation that she had talent and skill and wasn't trying to live out a hopeless dream that she had zero chance of achieving.

She kept them next to the TV as often the living room doubled as her office and she didn't want to lose sight of what mattered to her. She might be a horror movie blogger at the moment, but she was a filmmaker at heart. Those trophies acted as motivation. They were a reminder that she could do it, as the film had been a big deal for her. It had led to a couple of opportunities with various producers both over email and the odd one in person, but ultimately nothing had come from it.

Plenty of people had enjoyed the film, but she wasn't what they were looking for. It had been nice catching a glimpse of what lay ahead, but also a frustrating time with no kind of deal emerging from it. Still, these things don't happen overnight, and she was already in the midst of editing her next short primed to have another crack at it. After all, it was her dream to be a filmmaker, her destiny, and it had to start somewhere.

From the living room you could also see the sparse kitchen. The sides were empty barring a pile of dishes and plates. The bin was full and close to overflowing, while a recycling box stood beside it also filled to the brim with takeaway and microwave meal boxes. Other than said microwave there were no kitchen gadgets or cook books anywhere to be seen. A few basic utensils, some pots and pans, but that really was about it. Abby didn't cook, and especially didn't cook anything that hit that sweet spot between undercooked and burnt to a fucking crisp.

"Don't know how you can watch that shit!"

Abby twisted on the sofa to see her roommate Katie shaking her head behind her while dressed for a night out, or rather barely dressed in Abby's eyes. Katie continued her judgemental stare at both the shitty horror film on the TV, and her lazy roommate already in her pyjamas. She awaited Abby's response as the question wasn't rhetorical. She truly didn't understand how Abby could watch these type of nasty, depraved, vile movies.

Katie looked the complete opposite from Abby with lighter makeup and a more approachable vibe about her altogether. Big loopy earrings dangled from her lobes like they always did whether she was going out or not. She wore heels for nights out but normally preferred nice trainers. Her dress just about covered everything that needed to be covered but she certainly couldn't stretch for anything without compromising it. She didn't mind, she liked her body and had always been comfortable with it. Once again something wildly different from Abby who could never wear that dress in a million years.

Katie shook her head at the awful horror tropes that continued to blare from the TV.

"It's disgusting," she said flatly like it was an absolute stone cold fact.

"So is that dress," Abby instantly retorted.

Katie ignored the remark, "Why don't you ever watch anything normal?"

Before Abby could answer Psycho Hillbilly hammered Katie's point home as he closed in on the hapless Whitney again. "You ready to be stabbed with my pitchfork," he cackled at his awful innuendo.

Abby couldn't help but cringe, but no way was she letting Katie win this interaction.

They may have been roommates but the two women had nothing in common. Nothing whatsoever. They had nothing to talk about, so just argued. No common ground could break up the arguments, along with no nice things to say about each other to call a truce. The apartment was a constant battleground. Katie didn't care about the decoration of the apartment, she didn't mind the posters and trophies and stuff because she mostly lived in her bedroom. She didn't see this place as home, to her it was just a place to live so Abby could decorate it however she wanted. But if they could have an argument over something, anything, they would. And most of those arguments revolved around their respective lifestyles.

In Katie's defence she believed she was trying to help Abby, but Abby was never going to be the reality TV watching, going out clubbing type. Both were set in their ways, both judgemental, and both paid equal rent for the apartment so neither backed down. Katie was popular, tended to always have a smile, and got on with almost everyone. But her and Abby just couldn't connect in any way. Apparently they couldn't just ignore each other either.

The two had been roommates for four extremely long months now. Both moved into the place around the same time hoping their roommate would be easy to get along with after not quite being able to afford their own places yet. Both women were instantly disappointed. There was animosity from the start and that had only grown with their time together. Katie the sociable type, Abby not. Abby the creative weirdo, Katie the exactly what you see is what you get. Katie knew her place in the world, she was somewhat settled, and had a path laid out ahead of her. Abby on the other hand might have known what she wanted, but everything was always very uncertain and in a seemingly constant state of flux.

Abby really had thought that the short would be her breakthrough. Despite accepting that it wasn't, that it was another good step on a long journey, it had affected her mood for a while. It was hard not to. She'd consider different things, different approaches, different styles. She'd overthink and change too much, and then end up in exactly the same place she started because despite any self-doubt she was on the right path. Katie on the other hand would have a bad day, come home to a glass of wine, and then begin the next day afresh. A much healthier approach in her eyes, and maybe Abby's too.

Abby had ambitions of being a director, a producer, of running her own studio. She lived in the future all the time, almost dismissive of the blogs and good work she'd done while building towards that. Katie on the other hand happily worked as an apprentice hairdresser and took life daily while enjoying her weekends away from work. Both women worked equally hard as the other and were progressing in their fields at the same sort of rate but went about it in different ways. This again lead to them clashing like everything else. They'd argue even if they did both agree on something, but that was never going to happen.

"Normal is boring," Abby finally spurted out as she decided to keep the argument going. "Plus it's not always this bad, it's just these guys," she added waving her arms at the screen like Katie would know she was talking about the producing/ directing team known as the Splatploitation Brothers. She didn't.

Katie didn't wait for Abby to finish as she fired back.

"No, what's boring is staying in watching shitty horror films all the time. Come on Abby, come to Jealous instead. Live a little."

Abby instantly turned her nose up at the idea. She couldn't contain her disapproving laugh or smirk either, much to Katie's annoyance.

"What's wrong with Jealous?" Katie sharply asked.

"The name for starters," Abby replied with the same degree of sharpness as the two-faced off in a stare down once more. It was a typical Friday night for the pair with this argument playing out in various forms every weekend for the last four months.

Jealous was about as far from a place that Abby would go to as you could get. It was crammed for starters, and Abby didn't like crowds. She barely went to a supermarket. So the idea of being squeezed into a club like sweaty underdressed cattle didn't appeal to her at all. Then came the noise. Other people probably called it music, but not Abby. Noise. Excruciating noise. Made worse by the noise seemingly being continuous. Each lot of noise was thoroughly indistinguishable from the last.

Abby wasn't much of a drinker either. She didn't do drugs, and her flirting was embarrassing. Not that there'd be anyone in the club she'd want to flirt with. As for dancing, that was strictly off the table. Abby didn't enjoy it, couldn't do it, and was pretty sure that if she had a gun to her head and was told to dance she'd take the bullet. She tried going to a club once many years ago and found herself sitting in a corner somewhere at the back writing notes for a script she was working on. Needless to say her work colleagues at the time weren't impressed and Abby wasn't invited again. She considered that fact a victory.

Katie shook her head. It was useless, she gave up. Her attention turned away from the trash on the TV to the pile of dirty plates and dishes in the kitchen instead. A new target for her discontent towards Abby. "It's your turn to do the dishes."

Katie offered Abby a wicked stare but Abby wasn't paying attention. She was back scribbling on her notepad as she watched the over the top violence and cringeworthy sexist humour unfold on the TV.

"I said…" Katie repeated, but Abby interrupted before she finished.

"I haven't used any." It was Abby's turn to offer her own wicked stare but hers contained a flash of smugness about it as the never-ending arguments continued.

Katie tried her best to stamp her authority. "Just because you live out of cardboard boxes and cartons doesn't mean you don't have to help out."

"It does when none of them are mine," Abby replied without giving an inch.

Both women held their stares. Once again neither backing down. The film rumbled on in the background with an awful sound mix of screams, bad accents, and pigs. Seeing this would never end, Katie grabbed her leather jacket hanging from a hook in the living room. Time to go, but not before trying to get the last words in. "Enjoy another evening with your psychos and bimbos."

She stomped towards the door but couldn't get out in time without giving Abby the final say.

"Hey! Bimbo's are people too…" Abby started laughing at her own joke before she could even finish the sentence.

Katie took the opportunity to slam the front door as she left the apartment in a mood.

"Almost kept a straight face saying that," Abby told herself before spinning back to the TV.

Feet curled under her body, notepad in hand, she was ready for the garbage in front of her to unfold. The Splatploitation Brothers didn't disappoint as Abby stared at the TV with Whitney, covered in more blood, once again slowly trying to get away from the cackling stalking Psycho Hillbilly who closed in on her as she neared a pigpen…

Back On The Farm

Whitney toppled over the flimsy wooden railed fence that surrounding the pigsty after getting her foot stuck in the wire mesh. Mud splashed on to her already dirty face adding to the muck on her body and legs like she was wearing some form of camouflage. Unfortunately a Psycho Hillbilly hunted her, not a Predator, so all the mud succeeded in doing was making her feel even more fucking miserable. It tangled into her hair too, but that already looked far from its best and should have been the least of her concerns. Whitney was normally being very particular about her appearance, especially the aforementioned hair but now wasn't the time to worry about that.

She lay in the mud for a moment. Her whole body ached while her mind tried to keep up with the various thoughts and scenarios that ran through her head. She hadn't really had time to process any of them, but with that lunatic chasing her it probably wouldn't matter. She did her best not to think that way just yet. Whitney tried lifting herself up to continue the getaway but her body wouldn't comply. She felt spent. Every part of her ached. Every part of her was covered in mud. Every part of her felt bruised or numb. She looked broken, beaten, and weak. But despite all that, Whitney hadn't yet conceded defeat.

Whitney always had a certain defiance about her. She wasn't a clever girl, in fact it wouldn't be too harsh to call her dumb. She certainly told herself that enough. She wasn't particularly creative, or resourceful, and often was the last to get any joke told. She was at least sporty, in high school anyway, but it hadn't been particularly useful the older she got. It briefly helped during the beginnings of her escape, but now she had zero energy left so it didn't feel like any sort of advantage anymore. Despite all this however, there was one real trait she did have which could help her in any given situation, including this one - Whitney had heart. If she believed in something, or needed to succeed at something, she processed a kind of will power and drive most didn't.

If she was told she was wrong and Whitney knew she wasn't, she wouldn't back down. If she kept failing at something out of her grasp, she kept trying until she had nothing left. It didn't matter that often she didn't have the answer, or even enough knowledge to know where to find an answer, she kept on looking. For all her perceived weaknesses from overcritical types who looked down at Whitney, she had strength, often a lot more than they did. That heart was her strength, both in trying and succeeding in the things she had accomplished, and in being a kind generous person. She needed that heart, that strength, more than ever now though. The day had seriously taken its toll both mentally and physically on Whitney, and she was running on fumes.

Her eyes fell on a trough the opposite end of the pigsty. Whitney summoned any ounce of strength and energy she had left and dragged herself forward. She clawed herself closer and closer to the trough at the other end of the empty pen. There was nothing special about the trough. No real reason to head towards it, other than it was further from the farmhouse than she was now, and she had to get away. Baby steps, she thought with each crawl in a way she often did, but normally under less extreme circumstance. The pigs were all out collecting body parts it seemed, so for the briefest of moments Whitney crawled alone in some form of peace. A positive finally, as long as she didn't look behind her.

If Whitney had looked behind her she would have seen that Psycho Hillbilly had already made his way to the pen and that briefest moment of being alone was exactly that. Brief. He stepped carefully over the fence trying not to get caught on the mesh wire but still managed to snag himself. He started to wobble but kept upright. Any aura he had of being an unstoppable killing machine would have been somewhat broken in that moment if Whitney had seen it having previously given the impression that he could walk right through the fence like a total badass. If Abby had made the flick she'd have definitely cut that awkward tiptoeing out of the picture. It was kind of embarrassing.

Inside the pen, rather than marching straight for Whitney, Psycho Hillbilly circled around her to the trough. His first step had been towards her, but then he saw her goal and wanted some more fun. He knew she was done, so why not drag it out a little bit longer. Psycho Hillbilly wanted her to look up and see him at the trough. For her to know he stood there waiting for her, that he had won. That there's absolutely nothing she could do or could ever have done. That he was in complete and utter control and she was absolutely nothing, no-one. He could be a dick like that.

Whitney reached the trough without noticing him, therefore robbing him of his moment. But he didn't care. There was more than one way to humiliate her. She tried to use the trough to aid her climb back to a standing position still fully unaware that Psycho Hillbilly waited right in front of her. Her vision was blurred at this point, her mind scattered. Whitney could just about focus on the single task at hand, but other than that she was lost in thoughts of her dead friends, her further impending doom, and also she really could have been concussed. She hadn't noticed him enter the pen, let alone circle around in front of her. He had the drop on her. Now how best to use it?

Whitney tried to heave herself upwards using the trough for support when she caught a glimpse of something in front of her. Psycho Hillbilly didn't hesitate and took the opportunity to have just a little bit more fun with her before she registered it was him. He toppled the trough. The filthy dirty water drenched Whitney as the trough flipped over narrowly avoiding giving her another whack on the head. It sent her splashing to ground again as she lost her grip.

The shock of the water made her scream a different scream from all the recent frightened ones. This one was more like a scream you would let out when the water's too cold. Although in truth the water temperature wasn't the issue, more the fact that that asshole tipped it unexpectedly over her in the first place. It didn't help it was disgusting pig water either and smelt horrible. Water really isn't meant to have layer on top of it. Once again Psycho Hillbilly thought it was fucking hilarious, and from his perspective, it was.

"Now you're fit to roll with the pigs," he bellowed between his cruel laughs.

Whitney finally resigned to defeat. Lying face down in a pigsty covered in blood, mud, filthy dirty water, and probably pig shit, she'd run out of fight. Her friends were spread across the pavement in pieces and chunks. She'd been taunted, hit, and stabbed, all since she'd left the house, and a lot, lot worse inside it. She couldn't take anymore. Her body had shut down, it had simply taken too much, and her mind felt ready to completely snap. This was meant to be a fun trip to the countryside but had turned out to be anything but.

The five of them were meant to go out for a nice drive, find some lovely serene place to have a picnic, and gossip about various people they knew. Her friend Jess was going to tell them all about her new boyfriend while Alice would have no doubt started picking faults in him straight away. They'd get into a little argument about it before drinking some more and all getting along again. These were the days Whitney lived for. Just her, and her friends, being together and enjoying themselves. Nothing in the world could compare to that.

Whitney had particularly looked forward to seeing the stars up in the sky as the night rolled in, something she rarely got to do in the city. She was a city girl, and always would be, but she loved getting out into the countryside once in a while. That escape from the hectic day to day life of the city. She'd never retreat to the countryside to write a great novel or create some fantastic piece of art, or whatever other reasons people decided to retreat to these areas. But for her, getting to smell the flowers and walk in the wild grass was the little break she needed every now and then. She'd looked forward to this day all month.

But now Alice's head laid metres away from her body. Beth's too. And she couldn't even distinguish Jess and Hayley from the mess on the floor. Fuck knows what happened to their heads. All thoughts of the beautiful countryside and the mixture of smells and feelings which came with it had been replaced by unimaginable horror. The stench now were the sort of smells she'd never be able to get rid of as they drifted from the smears on the pavement that used to be her friends. Whitney didn't want to be a smear.

"Please don't hurt me," Whitney pleaded. "I'll do anything," she followed up a little less convincingly. She wouldn't be getting any of those awards Abby had on her shelf, that's for sure. Whitney slowly tried to make her way up from the mud once again. She didn't have much energy left and used most of it lifting her face from the floor, but somehow made it to her knees which led to a happy grin from Psycho Hillbilly. He was having the time of his life.

"Anything huh?" He said standing over her with his grin widening all the time. He pretended to mull over what possible things he could get her to do, but in truth he already knew. After all he was a sadistic Psycho Hillbilly slasher so he always had nasty thoughts in his head. Finally he looked down towards her with his menacing smile seeming to grow right off his ugly face.

"Lick my pitchfork."

*

Abby shook her head at the screen as she watched the awkwardness unfold. Her stomach started to rumble as Whitney leaned closer to the blood-soaked pitchfork. Chunks of flesh gruesomely glued to the fork knocked against her nose as she was mere inches away. A louder rumble escaped Abby's stomach. "Really, this can't be making you hungry," she jokingly said to her stomach. Her eyes flicked back to the screen as sucking sounds echoed from it. "Don't do it, girl," Abby shouted at the TV in a mocking fashion before her eyes drifted to a nearby pizza menu sitting on the coffee table.

She reached her notepad before the menu and frantically scribbled down some more notes. The gist of it was the same thing she had written every time she watched a Splatploitation Brothers movie. 'Yet another dumb female character that is only good for showing her tits and being in a position to make a blowjob joke.'

"Swear I've seen this scene in every one of their movies," she muttered before underlining the paragraph far more than necessary.

Snatching the menu she glanced up in time to watch Psycho Hillbilly stick the pitchfork right through Whitney's petrified face. It pieced the bottom of her rubbery-looking mouth with ease. After a slight delay blood began to pour from the mouth, too much blood. Whitney gagged as vomit mixed with blood to the tune of Abby's still rumbling stomach, and somewhat disgusted face.

"Can't tell if that's a good effect or not," she told herself as she flicked through the menu while keeping her eyes on the screen.

She always had mixed feelings about the practical effects in a Splatploitation Brothers flick. Some looked downright awful, straight out of an Ed Wood movie, while others were actually quite convincing and almost felt real. She liked that they used practical effects, that they'd never gone near CGI. That was their one positive in Abby's book, not that she'd ever give them credit for it, or anything else.

Abby enjoyed trashing the Splatploitation Brothers in her reviews. Their movies didn't deserve any praise in her eyes, even when parts of them were passable. She knew it wasn't the most professional approach, but her job as she saw it was to give her opinion, and her overriding opinion of the Splatploitation Brothers was that they sucked. Still, she considered mentioning this one good effect, but it really didn't make up for all the poor ones.

Pieces of Whitney's face slid to the floor with the newly arrived pigs hungrily waiting beneath. It was unclear what exact part of the face they were meant to be but the pigs were enjoying them nonetheless. They were not fussy eaters. Abby made a point of telling herself no bacon on the pizza. After a hard cut the pitchfork now somehow stuck from the ground with what remained of Whitney's severed head impaled on it. The rest of her body slowly slummed to the ground giving the pigs even more food to devour in what was possibly another good effect which Abby would in no way give them credit for. Mostly she'd give them no credit for it because the sequence made absolutely no sense whatsoever. In fairness it was a trashy B-Movie slasher flick so would normally be forgiven, but not by Abby when it's a Splatploitation Brothers movie.

Psycho Hillbilly revved up a chainsaw that appeared from absolutely fucking nowhere and narrowed in on the remains of Whitney's headless body. "Hey Ma, get the barbecue sauce ready," he squawked in that ridiculous accent once more.

So no BBQ either, Abby thought before Psycho Hillbilly cut into Whitney's tits. "We got us some juicy meat," he cackled slipping back into something that sounded somewhat closer to awful Irish than awful Southern. Abby added no boobs to her list, but luckily no such thing existed on the menu she continued to examine while Psycho Hillbilly gleefully chopped Whitney into several more pieces.

The Blog

The title card repeated continuously on the menu screen with the film long since over. Every twenty seconds 'Hillbilly Farm' would flash up on the TV in bright thick red letters with gore dripping from the words into the silhouetted shape of a farmhouse below. A screaming sound normally accompanied it, but Abby had at least got as far as muting the damn thing. She always left the menu playing in the background when she finished a film. Something that annoyed Katie immensely, and probably a good reason for Abby to do it, if it wasn't something she used to do at her old digs all the time already.

It had become part of her process over the years. She'd leave the title screen up there as a way of keeping the film fresh in her mind while she wrote her review. The films nowadays didn't tend to have clips in the title screen like they used too. Abby missed that, but she'd kept the practice out of habit anyway. It was only in recent years that she'd started muting it. Once upon a time she wouldn't have, the same twenty second soundbite would have repeated over and over for hours. But she just couldn't handle that anymore. She wasn't sure what had changed, but something had. Katie would have been extremely grateful for the change had she ever had to live through the original film watching aftermath.

Abby stood at the door to the apartment taking a huge cheese pizza off the delivery guy. By the end of *Hillbilly Farm* she'd decided against meat that night. It wasn't that they'd scared her off it, more just put her off it for the evening with their cringeworthy humour. The delivery guy was a nice guy. Younger than Abby by a year or two, a bit of a slacker, but he always had a friendly smile. Most importantly, as far as Abby was concerned, he always delivered her pizzas on time, even if the same couldn't be said by his other customers.

Brushing his floppy hair from his eyes he peered into the apartment towards the television spotting the *Hillbilly Farm* writing sprawled across the screen. He smiled in recognition of the film. One he'd seen himself, and enjoyed, despite it being totally shit from any kind of artistic viewpoint. Unlike Abby he loved the bad movies the Splatploitation Brothers produced, could see plenty of merit in them in terms of effort and having fun. They were entertaining, even if not to everyone's taste. He liked the posters up on her wall too, the classics of the genre, but could also happily watch what Abby would consider total garbage. Not that she hated trashy movies, just *their* trashy movies. Something about them.

"You going to be nice to them this time?" He nodded towards the TV but Abby already knew what he meant as they'd discussed horror films plenty in the past.

She always hoped he'd be the guy delivering the pizza, and he often was. Abby liked to think it was because he saw her order pop up on the screen and rushed over take it but knew that was unlikely. They probably had some system where someone else issued all the orders and he just happened to be designated to this area. Still, it was a nice daydream which put a smile on her face because she really did think he was cute and liked that he watched plenty of movies.

Abby had often thought that maybe one day they could go and watch a film together. Maybe find some nice coffee or cake shop afterwards and chat about the movie while they enjoyed their refreshments. She always liked those scenes in movies. Imagined having a partner she could chat to about the particulars in a scene, or how the lighting conveyed a certain mood. She had a chance to talk like that in university, and still could with her blog, but she missed the conversation part of it. Despite being somewhat antisocial and definitely not a people person she had needs, and Abby's needs were to passionately discuss cinema.

She shook her head, "You been reading my blog?" She asked knowingly.

"Always," he replied with his charming smile.

Abby loved that smile. She'd never admit that to him, or sometimes even herself, but she really did like his smile a lot. She thought he knew he had a great smile too, but it wasn't really something you could say to someone or ask them about. Least she thought you couldn't. She hadn't really tried because well, she'd feel awkward and would most definitely make a fool of herself. Not that she gave a shit what others thought, except maybe him. Another thing she'd never admit.

"Then you know I'm not going to be nice to them," she finally replied in a flirty tone, or rather her attempt at flirty after being captured in his smile for a moment too long.

"I think they're getting better," he fondly replied with sincerity.

"And that's why you're delivering pizza and not critiquing films," Abby bluntly replied and instantly regretted. She didn't mean it, at least she thought she didn't. But she had said it as clear as day and he'd heard both in her words, and her tone, that she did in fact mean it. His lovely smile faded.

Any sense of flirting was over at that point. The moment completely and utterly gone. The delivery guy, who Abby thought was called Ben but couldn't quite be sure and was too embarrassed to ask again, just stood there. He wasn't really sure how to respond, and Abby was too busy wallowing in her awkwardness. She handed over the cash while staring at the floor trying her best not to visibly curse herself. Ben, if that was his real name, for his part gave her a polite goodbye and told her to enjoy her evening. But even that felt forced and uncomfortable after Abby's rudeness.

He seemed like he really wanted to say something back to her, probably tell her how uncool that was, but he didn't. Whether it was fear for his job, as arguing with customers was most definitely frowned upon no matter how they acted, or whether it was because he liked her back and she'd hurt his feelings, Abby would never know. She closed the door as he left and leant against it.

"What is wrong with me?" She ruefully asked herself fighting the urge to run after him and apologise, which being such a nice guy he'd gladly have accepted. But she didn't.

Abby's history with guys was full of instances like this. Anyone she remotely liked, which wasn't that many people to begin with, she'd always manage to insult before things had even really got started. She'd laugh at something they wore or put them down in front of their friends over absolutely nothing. Or find some other way to be completely unnecessarily flat out rude. She couldn't be sure why she done it. She tried to convince herself it was a defence mechanism to make sure she stayed single and free of responsibility while she worked on her career, but she knew that was a lie. If the right person came along, she could do both, plenty of people surely did.

The truth of the matter as far as Abby could really tell was she was just outright shit at talking to people, just fucking appalling at it. The worst. Certainly most people who met her would back up that claim. But she wasn't happy with being that way. Sure she liked her independence and everything and did enjoy her own company more than that of others, but still, it wouldn't hurt to have a friend. Maybe even a partner every once and a while. She hated at times how judgemental and rude she could be, but she was trying to work on that. Mostly she thought of it as a defensive reflect, something she used on people that wronged her first. But every now and again it came out at the wrong time, and normally that wrong time was when she was speaking to someone she actually liked.

She made a promise to herself that she would apologise to Ben(?) next time she saw him. After all she instantly knew that she had been rude, and still hadn't taken it back. On the other hand he had still been kind enough to wish her a good evening and hadn't trampled over her pizza or called her names like she would most definitely have done. Plus there was that smile, that cheeky and handsome at the same time smile of his.

Abby had made up her mind. For the first time, in a long time, she'd apologise for something. The thought that maybe she could savage that imaginary film and cake date sprang back into her mind and made her smile. It was instantly wiped out however with the, 'well you shouldn't have been a bitch to him because that ain't going to happen now,' thought that followed. Stupid brain. At least she could console herself with a huge cheese pizza all to herself. One of the bonuses of single life, and an abnormally high metabolism.

Abby brought the pizza to the coffee table and grabbed her laptop from the small shelf compartment underneath it. She set herself up for what remained of the night with the pizza box sitting open and the laptop at the ready. Abby logged onto her site ready to write her latest review as she took a large bite of her cheese pizza. The *Hillbilly Farm* logo continued to loop on the TV in front of her.

The site, called 'Abby versus horror,' was a personal blog site she used to review horror films. She'd made a bit of a name for herself with it over the last four years and had a nice sized following. The independent directors and producers of the films she reviewed generally always checked her posts and hoped for a favourable one. Abby however did not give praise away lightly, you had to earn it. She couldn't be brought off with premier tickets or merchandise and wasn't trying to buddy up to the system with favourable reviews in the hopes of them acknowledging her. Abby was honest with her critiques, she had integrity. Bottom line, she'd always tell you how she felt about your movie whether you liked that honesty or not. So far the Splatploitation Brothers had never earned any praise from Abby, not even close. In fact she may not have ever printed one single nice word about them.

Hillbilly Farm was not going to be the exception. She wasted no time making that clear as she began her latest blog entry:

"The Splatploitation Brothers once again splattered the screen with blood, gore, and more sexist masturbation-inducing trash".

Abby continued hammering away on the keyboard as she devoured the massive pizza forgetting her delivery guy woes and taking her failed flirting frustrations out on the deserved target in her mind. The Splatploitation Brothers.

The Splatploitation Brothers

The interior of a log cabin bedroom for the Splatploitation Brothers latest horror flick, *"Return of Doctor Breaker,"* sat on a small sound stage. The set itself looked rather cheap, but nonetheless passible if you didn't look too hard. The plywood walls had been crudely painted to resemble a log cabin while the roughly cut carpet on the floor didn't sit right at all. They'd put a window frame on one of the walls with curtains to hide the nothingness that hid it. A second-hand thin bed had been assembled with a heavy duvet spread over the top to give it the more homely feel you'd associate with a cabin. A single empty bookcase stood beside it.

They didn't need anything else as the camera had been set up to capture the best angle of the set rather than tell the story. Overall it didn't look great, but making independent features while shooting on film required certain cost cutting sacrifices. Plus it was their style to have plain interior sets and by this point was considered a Splatploitation Brothers trademark.

The sound stage itself was located in an old previously abandoned two-story fire station on the ground floor. The upper floor of the building where the sleeping quarters for the firemen once were, was now the bedrooms of the Splatploitation Brothers, complete with a bathroom and small kitchen. On the ground floor stood the sound stage, along with a couple of equipment rooms, prop rooms, an office, and another small kitchen. The basement of the building was off limits to everyone except the Splatploitation Brothers. In fact most people, i.e everyone who wasn't a Splatploitation Brother, didn't even know there was a basement.

Lying on the bed within the log cabin set were two half-naked actresses both waiting for their cues. They lay side by side partially under the duvet. Both actresses were in their late twenties but playing teens in what could probably be considered a horror convention at this point. Neither were very good actors, but they didn't have to be on a Splatploitation Brother set. Mandy had long flowing black hair, while Beth's was blonde meaning both matched the extremely vague description of their characters in the script that read 'teens, one with black hair, one with blonde.' In truth Mandy's hair was brown but she wanted the role so dyed it knowing that the wrong colour hair would be a deal breaker in a Splatploitation Brothers feature. They could be fickle like that.

"Action," was yelled from the front of the set.

The two girls started kissing passionately on the bed as the cameraman slowly pushed in. Both tried their hardest to get into the right mood despite the set having a rather unprofessional feel about it with the small crew all eagerly leering over the actresses. As they began to move about under the sheets a script fell from the bed. Both actresses immediately noticed and stopped. They looked rather embarrassed by the blunder and tried their best not to laugh at the silly mistake. If they'd had carried on all would have been fine, these kind of thing happens in a Splatploitation Brothers flick as film is expensive and continuity always came second to shot footage, but as they stopped the take was ruined. An annoyed, "cut," was shouted by the director.

While the rather nice old school bulky film camera they'd managed to pick up was being reset the director, and leader of the Splatploitation Brothers, Percy Clement sat impatiently in his personalised director's chair. In his late thirties now he'd been in the horror game for well over half his life. He'd directed over forty films, although only in the last few years had the budgets risen above zero and the quality above Z Grade. Percy always sported a horror t-shirt and a shabby director's beard, an image that he'd very purposefully cultivated for himself. It wasn't a great look on him, but that's not what he thought, and no one was going to tell him otherwise. In his eyes he looked like one of the great maverick filmmakers of the seventies when films were films.

He saw his own films in that manner too. None of this CGI bullshit, he'd say. The sets were made or shot on location. There was bare minimum green screen if any at all. The effects were all practical, in camera, and everything was shot on film stock including the behind the scenes stills. This was a studio that made horror films in the now, but with the aesthetic and gear of the video nasties from the seventies and eighties. He always liked to capture the spirit of those movies too. Percy was rather proud of these facts, and quite frankly should be. He thoroughly believed that if you were making a horror film and didn't offend anyone, then you hadn't done your job.

"For fuck sake, someone get that script out the way."

A runner darted to the bed picking the script up from the floor. He missed it at first as his eyes stayed on the half-naked actresses in front of him for a moment too long. Unfortunately that was the attitude at times on the Splatploitation Brothers sets. It wasn't one they actively encouraged, but one that happened nonetheless. They'd had a lot of the same basic crew for a long time and it had become a little clique-like and unprofessional behind the scenes. Both actresses gave the runner an unfriendly look back but in his eyes it was totally worth it. He dashed out of view of the camera as Percy sat looking anything but impressed with this break in shooting. With everybody out the way they started again.

"And action!"

The actresses both stared directly at the camera not ready for the restart. The sound guy also wasn't ready as the boom mic sat in full view within the shot. They all quickly fell into position with Percy's patience seriously waning as the clapperboard operator also frantically changed the take number.

"Can we all start showing some fucking professionalism!" Percy snapped at everyone on set.

"Action," he abruptly announced once more. The camera operator, who had stopped filming when Percy began to talk, taking that as a cut, now had to quickly start rolling again without him noticing. He had heard how camera operators tended to not last long on Percy's set but needed the job and couldn't risk irritating him. That seemed to be the one position that wasn't included in the tight knit crew as Percy always looked down on their work after each shoot. He hoped he hadn't missed the beginning of the scene but knew he'd fail to capture the quickly done clapperboard. What a mess.

The two actresses embraced once again. They started fooling around under the covers giving the performance everything they had.

"Oh Mandy, I've been waiting to experiment all spring break."

"Me too Beth."

Unfortunately for them the dialogue left a lot to be desired and everything they had wasn't much to begin with. But still, everyone was trying their best, and Percy seemed happy as he nodded along to the performance in front of him. The camera operator moved in for their close up.

Both looked up in a terribly cliché manner as the camera reached its mark.

"Did you hear something?" Beth unconvincingly asked.

They stared awkwardly into the distance before resuming their kissing dismissing the none existing sound that would become an actual faint sound in post. Their bodies locked together under the sheets. The crew all eagerly watched. Percy mouthed along to every word the actresses spoke nodding his approval at his own wonderful dialogue.

"All I can hear is the sound of our love," Mandy finally answered woodenly.

Percy wiped his right eye like there was a tear coming from it. Beautiful. God he loved being a writer director. An auteur. A master of his craft in his not so humble completely biased opinion.

A shadow started to appear behind the 'teens' on the log cabin wall. The cameraman pulled back slightly and panned away from the action on the bed to reveal the titular Mad Scientist Doctor Breaker entering the frame all the while being careful not to show too much of the set that side. The Doctor wore the traditional get up you'd expect from a Mad Scientist. The white lab coat, the black trousers, goggles. His hair was spiked and silver and his face looked remarkably like the Psycho Hillbilly, mostly because they were being played by the same person. Another member of the Splatploitation Brothers, Matthew Speedman.

He carried a small knife in his hand shaped to look like a hypodermic needle. It wasn't the most convincing of props, but points still had to be given for creativity. The camera tracked Matthew while still being careful not to reveal the undressed side of the cabin set as he crept towards the raunchy couple. The girls continued to squirm under the bedsheets as Matthew reached them. He lifted the hypodermic knife high above his head twisting the lab coat a little in the process so it floated in an imaginary wind for a second before he readied to bring the knife down when…

… A fake bloody breast prop popped up from under the sheets right in view of the camera, Matthew, and the onlooking crew that included Percy.

"Fuck," whispered Beth from under the bedsheets.

"Cut! This is getting ridiculous."

The set was a whirlwind of activity as the crew started resetting the camera position and reapplying makeup after Percy called a halt to the scene.

Roger Coles walked towards the prop. Picking it up he gave it the once over before he looked back to Percy informing him it wasn't damaged. Roger was the third member of the Splatploitation Brothers and easily the most laid back. He made all the effects and props used in their flicks and also helped out with the cinematography from time to time. However the effects and props were definitely more his wheelhouse.

He was a big guy, heavy set, easily the biggest dude in any given room. Whatever he wore was normally covered in fake blood, latex, or some other liquid used within his props. His top was always too short on him so his gut seemed forever on display. He was a hard worker though, and not bad at what he did either, although he always believed he never got the appreciation he deserved from either his Splatploitation Brothers colleagues or the outside world.

Roger had fallen in love with special effects after watching *American Werewolf in London* and the original *Dawn of the Dead*. Like many working in the effects department his heroes were Rick Baker and Tom Savini. He worked every day to be like them and while he wasn't close, and probably never would be, that didn't stop his child-like wonder at creating effects and solving problems. He was a huge asset to the Splatploitation Brothers whether they told him that or not.

Roger shook his head disapprovingly at the actresses despite the prop being ok. Both looked at him in an apologetic manner but he was already over it and moving on to the next thing. Roger may have had many faults, but holding a grudge wasn't one of them. That was Matthew's department. Matthew stormed off set nearly tripping over a light in the process.

"Fuck Matthew, watch it!" Percy barked as Matthew held a

staring contest with the light stand. His attention turned to Percy at the mention of his real name.

"What have I told you about talking to me like that. Bet De Niro never got that from Scorsese, or Bale from…"

Percy interrupted him like he always did to anyone speaking when he wanted to speak. "That's cos De Niro doesn't fall over the lights does he? He's a professional."

"You want to talk about professionalism," Matthew cried while pointing at the two actresses. "I'm leaving everything up there in front of the camera. I'm baring my heart and soul and they can't even keep hold of a goddamn prop." He marched towards the craft service table while muttering away to himself.

"This is the first time I've broken character all week," he said turning back towards Percy and unleashing the most dramatic of dramatic points: "And that's on your head."

Matthew reached the craft table and scanned the biscuit range only to became even more enraged. "Damn it! Who ate all the Jammie Dodgers?" He gave the table a swift kick like it was the tables fault before hobbling away to sulk in a corner. Nobody checked on Matthew as this sort of scene was pretty frequent. Matthew was, and always would be, a complete and utter diva. His tantrums were legendary within certain circles and anyone who had worked with him had witnessed them at least a couple of times. He took his acting extremely seriously seeing himself as a modern day Lon Chaney, but in reality he was much closer to Joey Tribbiani.

The last of the Splatploitation Brothers was Duncan Turner, the oldest of the four sneaking into his forties while the rest were late thirties. Slim, with square framed glasses and greasy hair he didn't have the loud personality and overenthusiastic disposition of the other three and saw himself more as the clever quiet one of the group.

He was considered the producer of the films and was often

in charge of pre-production. He got everything ready up until the shoot began, and sometimes during if it was something Percy didn't want to deal with. He worked his magic on the budgets, call sheets, any necessary insurance and licences, and location scouted when they needed it. Like Roger he wasn't bad at his job, but not great either. What he really wanted to do was direct, but he hadn't had that chance yet. He had a Sci-Fi B-Movie script that he'd been working on for ten years but it had never made the Splatploitation Brothers slate with Percy always seemingly having his next project ready to go. He sat beside Percy glaring at his laptop like he normally did on set. "Review's up."

Before Percy could reply Roger was in his ear and Duncan was instantly forgotten about. Just like Matthew's tantrums this was normally the case on a Splatploitation Brothers set. The four had been friends ever since college and always would be despite clashing all the time. They were a team of filmmakers who had combined their powers to make their own so-called studio and produce a bunch of horror films every year. They had their fans and following and knew that together they were better than apart. Still, Duncan wished that every now and then they'd pay attention to him.

Roger waved the hypodermic needle knife prop in front of Percy.

"I think we should make it bigger."

"Do you?" Percy sarcastically replied. "Well what about all the other scenes it's already been used in."

"He could have made it bigger since then. We've shot chronologically so far."

"I like it being small, it's more…"

"Personal," Duncan said interjecting himself into the conversation.

Roger finally realised that Duncan was sitting beneath them.

"This isn't your department Duncan," he bluntly stated.

Duncan's eyes dropped from the conversation back to his laptop.

Roger held the knife in his hand still examining it. It looked small in his hands, but then most things did. "I feel like this would break if I stabbed someone with it. I want it to look fucking mean."

Percy stared blankly at Roger. "It's a hypodermic needle that's a knife. It is fucking mean."

Roger gazed at the knife still unsure. "Yeah it's mean. I just want it to look mean as well."

Duncan gasped below them as he scanned through the review. Neither paid any attention to him.

"Roger this is your invention," Percy remarked getting tired of the conversation.

"I can do better is what I'm saying," Roger instantly replied.

"We're halfway through the shoot. The knife is in every scene."

"We can add a scene of him constructing a new knife," Roger replied even quicker with a smile on his face like he'd solved everything.

Percy wasn't impressed. He coldly stared at Roger like some great insult had occurred between the two of them, and in Percy's eyes, it had.

"Are you writer director?"

Roger shook his head.

"Then there is no 'we' when it comes to my script."

Roger nodded in agreement, although he couldn't keep quiet for long.

"I just think…"

"Well next time think it sooner," Percy interrupted in typical Percy fashion.

Duncan stood up between them with his hand over his

mouth. Percy and Roger finally gave him the attention he craved. "What's up with you?" they both asked together.

Percy glanced at the laptop screen and saw Abby's review. "Everyone take five," he announced to the room.

The Review

The four Splatploitation Brothers sat around an enormous wooden table in their smallish office. There wasn't much room for anything else in the office with the oversized table, but they were ok with that. They loved their big dramatic table. It made them feel important. They could still get to their chairs, so that's all they cared about. The walls were plastered with horror posters to the point where there was no telling what the original colour of the wall had been. The office was the first room they had set up when they moved into the building three years ago. Slowly they had built up the other rooms to what they were now, but this was the first room they had decorated combining all their separate posters and horror tastes into one room. This was the brains of the Splatploitation Brothers Studio operation. The war room.

Back then they'd only just started to create a small following and wanted to expand the Splatploitation Brothers Production name into more of a Studio. They had looked at several office buildings they couldn't possibly afford and a few warehouses that didn't really fit their needs before laying eyes on the abandoned fire station. Not only was it a good size and space, and just about within their price range if they all pulled together and had some ok success with their next few films, but also it was an abandoned fire station just like the Ghostbusters. How could they not get it?

After they had decorated the office and brought a table they absolutely loved and believed fitted into the small office but really was actually far too big they shot their first film as a Studio called 'The Vicious Mutants of Splatterville Fire Station.' They used the small traces of the buildings past as production value and had even managed to get an old fire engine inside as a prop. As always, not a very good one considering it was more of a fire van that had limited in case of emergency use and it ended up being rarely shown in the poorly made and reviewed film. *The Vicious Mutants of Splatterville Fire Station* was the last of the no budget Splatploitation Brothers films as they took a somewhat more professional approach after that despite the quality still lacking in some people's eyes.

They had planned to use the massive amount of money they thought they'd make from the flick to build their own sound stage. Unfortunately the film sold for barely thousands rather than multi-millions, but then Percys Grandad died and left him a fair amount of money so that made up the difference. From then on the fire engine space was converted to the small sound stage they now used and the big bay doors were locked shut with blackout sheets placed over them.

Percy never held that investment over the group. Largely he didn't need to as he always got what he wanted anyway, but more because that just wasn't how they worked. That money was for the studio and they were all part of that studio. The greater good. While money was always tight for them and their various productions one of the better things about the group was none of them truly cared about money. They were all legitimately in the business to make the best horror movies they could and just meant they might have a better budget for the next one. It was refreshing and kind of sweet.

All four had horror mugs sitting in from of them on the large table. A Splatploitation Brothers tradition which had existed since the early college days when they'd sit around arguing about various horror movies while downing a ton of coffee. Percy had a *Wizard of Gore* mug, Roger had a *Braindead* one, Duncan's was *The Thing*, while Matthew had gone for a *Re-Animator* mug. Matthew was still in costume so sat cross-legged on the chair in his mad scientist outfit as Duncan began to read

Abby's latest review from this laptop.

"The Splatploitation Brothers once again splattered the screen with blood, gore, and more sexist masturbation-inducing trash".

Roger nodded his approval at the opening lines. So far so good. Percy and the others weren't so favourable however. Abby had never given them a good review in the past and this wasn't sounding any different. The group was aware that like them she also had a loyal following that hung on her every word and a bad review, they always felt, affected sales. While that probably wasn't true, they would have still liked it if she said something nice about them, even if none of them would admit that. Duncan continued:

"Their latest offering Hillbilly Farm forgoes all that makes the slasher genre so interesting and instead tries to fit in as much gore, scanty clad teens, and awkward dialogue as inhumanly possible."

Roger continued to nod his approval. It sounded like his kind of slasher flick, and it quite literally was. Matthew stood up, started pacing in the limited space while muttering quietly to himself. Duncan looked to Percy for what to do next. Percy gestured for him to continue.

"Director Percy Clements seems even more at lost with the camera than his last weak blood soaked cringe-fest, 'Gore Girls of Slasher Beach.' The repetitive nature of his master, mid, close shooting and editing style suggests after forty-plus films he's still working his way through the Dummies Guide to Directing. I'm also hoping one day he'll realise he doesn't just have to point the camera at blood and tits, but then I thought that fifteen films back and nothing has changed."

"Well who doesn't love blood and tits? Sounds like a compliment to me," Roger happily said aloud to the room. Matthew's pacing intensified. He'd never been one to handle reviews, or opening nights, or anything really. This wasn't any different.

"Fuck sake Matthew! Sit down," Percy ordered trying his

best not to show his own immediate frustration at the review so far. Matthew ignored him. Duncan gave Percy a look he'd had to give many times before when Matthew was in character like this. When he was Daniel Day Lewising it until the final shot was in the can. Percy hated that look, or rather what that look meant, but if they wanted to move things forward he had no choice but to give in as Matthew could be more stubborn than even he could

Percy gave in, "Doctor Breaker, sit down."

Matthew sat as Percy waved Duncan on to continue once more. Duncan looked apologetically towards Matthew as he began the next portion of the review.

"Always leading man Matthew Speedman may have topped his own worse performance with his laughable accent, ridiculous look, and shameful rapey humour. How is he getting worse? Surely being the worst actor ever is enough, why aim lower? But lower he aims, and nails it every single time. Has to be time to pack it in and get a paper round or something by now."

Roger carried on nodding in agreement, not that anyone in the room noticed. Matthew had thrown back his chair and jumped to his feet almost destroying his mug in the process. Again he unleashed one of his overly dramatic points, this time aimed at the laptop.

"This slanderous jealous attack has to…"

"Sit down Matthew," Percy interjected once more as Matthew readied to burst into tears.

"Sit down Doctor Breaker," he reluctantly followed it with not wanting to make things worse.

Matthew steadied himself enough ready to burst into another rant as Percy began to lose patience. Before he'd even got halfway through yet another dramatic point that was seemingly becoming a trademark of 'Doctor Breaker' Percy intervened once more.

"Don't make me ask you again," he coldly stated.

Matthew grabbed his chair from the floor and retook his place as he continued his sulk. Duncan skipped a few more paragraphs of Matthew bashing correctly surmising he wouldn't be able to handle anymore and reached the next section of the review instead.

"Once again effects supervisor Roger Coles takes centre stage over the, and I use the term loosely, story. Much like Matthew's acting everything looked ridiculously fake. I think it's about time they replace him with an app as I'm sure there must be some out there that make more realistic effects and demand less attention."

"What a bitch," Roger shouted with his nodding coming to a sudden halt.

Duncan skipped a bunch more sections that basically trashed their movie, them, and some of the types of people that watch their films, before reading the conclusion aloud.

"While the Splatploitation Brothers will always have their fans they continue to fail to make it to the next level. They remain below ground in a pit of unrealistic gore, bad puns, terrible acting, and an ever increasing disgraceful portrayal of women. I think it's safe to say at this point that none of them have any understanding of filmmaking, or women, whatsoever."

Duncan closed the laptop as Percy abruptly left the room without saying a word. The remaining three stayed quiet for a moment. They were all use to brutal reviews, especially from Abby as she never gave them anything but, but this one felt personal. She used to just say they were shit and she didn't like the film, but this was different. The naming and shaming of each individual member of the group was something new. It was an attack. She was trolling them in their eyes, and to a degree they were right. Abby would never think anyone on a filmset should be replaced by an app but she knew it sounded funny in a mean-spirited way and couldn't help herself.

Duncan was the first to speak trying to put a positive spin on the ugly review.

"Well I think that was a more positive review than *Gore Girls*…" he started to lie.

Roger wasn't going to let him finish. "It started well then turned shit," he abruptly interjected still very much stewing over her app crack at him. He could understand the Matthew jabs even though he thought as an outsider she had no right to take the piss out of Matthew. That was reserved for them only. But he knew his effects were damn decent. In his eyes that wasn't a boast, it was fact.

Matthew gave his few cents in between the sobs. "How can she say my accent was laughable. I spent months working on that. That was a genuine Psycho Hillbilly slasher accent."

Duncan and Roger both give Matthew a comforting pat on the back. Whatever either thought privately about some of Matthew's acting at times they were both his friends and knew how much effort he put into his roles. He didn't deserve such a review no matter how right she was about the horribly nauseating accent.

"She doesn't know real film making…" Matthew started to say with his face reddening.

"I think you done great Matt. Nailed it," Roger said, seeing Matthew was close to bursting again.

Matthew smiled at the pair forgetting for a brief moment that he was still meant to be in character under his own rules. He knew she was just jealous. That had to be what it was. Otherwise… no, there was no otherwise. It was jealously pure and simple Matthew thought while sucking up the tears and doing his best to not directly look at anyone.

Percy re-entered the office and slid an old small defunct looking Super 8 camera across the large table.

"We have our new leading lady," he ruefully announced.

Late Night Edit

Abby sat alone in her hoodie and jeans in the modern editing suite at her old university. Her eyes were glued to the two monitors in front of her as one began to play. The screen showed a beautifully framed huge concrete bridge as haunting music softly played over the top of the image and the title credit gently faded in, *'Suicide Bridge.'* It all looked very professional as Abby watched it through again.

She had finished at the university two years beforehand passing with a first but was allowed back on campus when she was editing a short film and the suites were free. She wasn't given priority, but always seemed to be able to book one. She often thought, and maybe correctly so, that the other kids just weren't as dedicated as her. Unlike a lot of them she had not gone to university for the social life. She was one hundred percent about learning as much as possible during her time there and any social life she had partaken in was purely accidental.

Abby got on well with her professors and the whole media department in general. She was the darling pupil during her time and always loved long conversations and debates about films. She clashed with them a lot over certain movies, but always considered their opinions. She may be rude to people her own age, but she was respectful of her elders for the most part. She often popped back into the university to check how everyone was doing even when she didn't have a project on the go. The professors and the media department were one of the few areas in her life she did have time for. She had made a point of thanking the department plenty for the awards that had come her way and had included them in the credits with a thank you too. She had also named the various professors as producers.

Abby was forever grateful for their teachings.

The editing suite itself was beautiful. One of the best in the country outside of a film studio, and one of the main reasons Abby decided to go to this particular university. There were eight editing suites in total, all with the latest video editing boards and 4K monitors. There was a superb sound mixing desk and a microphone for any additional ADR. The video control panel was slick and intuitive and Abby loved every second she got to spend with it. This suite, or one of the seven identical ones, had become Abby's happy place. After a few years of using the ultra-modern, and super-efficient suite at the university there was no way she could go back to editing on her dated laptop.

Abby played through the scene on the monitor once more. A very slow crawl on an old massive concrete bridge that lead to a city at dusk where the titles gently faded in like they were coming from the softly illuminated sky. She was happy with the result. Like her last movie this one was a ghost story too, but Abby felt it was a massive step forward from the previous effort. She'd grown as a filmmaker in her eyes over the last year and had a better grasp of how to tell the story exactly how she wanted. She'd matured. Had a finer eye for detail and a better understanding of what worked and why. Abby looked at the opening once more allowing herself a moment to imagine the film festival laurel wreaths and five-star reviews running along the bottom of the image. A lovely daydream and one she was determined to make a reality.

She took a swig from the coffee cup sat at her side but the cup was empty. Editing time had struck again. She'd actually finished the coffee two hours ago, but to her it had felt like ten minutes. Abby thought she'd been adding the finishing touches to the opening credits for an hour, but it had been closer to four in total. Like a Vegas casino floor with no clocks or windows, time just flowed differently when editing and she loved it. You could lose yourself in it. The one place her brain was ultra-focused. No other thoughts crept in. Inside the editing room it was simple, just the task at hand and how to solve whatever problem came up. The current problem consisted of a lack of caffeine as she placed the empty cup beside the other two.

*

Abby stood at the hot drinks dispenser in the empty university corridor. She slid her coins into the machine and made the quick decision to go for regular filtered coffee. She wasn't one for any kind of fancy coffee. She'd tried them all at some stage or another wanting to be a coffee connoisseur who seemed to have their own winning combination not on the menu, but it wasn't meant to be. None of them really did anything for her. Turned out just good old-fashion filtered coffee was the one for Abby. The dispenser began to make some odd sounds like it was deciding whether it should make the coffee or not. It was one of the only things in the building that wasn't relatively new.

The university itself was an old building despite all the modern equipment inside. Many years ago they had contemplated building a new facility but instead decided to renovate what they had and keep the old aesthetic. So the old building remained with a bit of a facelift and some structural work to fix any issues. It was then stuffed full of the latest and greatest teaching aids and equipment, barring the coffee machine apparently. It attracted great professors, but that, alongside the renovations, all led to a hefty price tag to enrol and live by. Abby took the chance and never regretted it, but it was the reason she now couldn't afford to rent her own place and had to share with Katie.

A lot of the other students from Abby's year had taken runner jobs for various film companies or had gone into areas around what they wanted to do after graduation, but Abby had no intention of doing that. She wanted to create her own path. Her blog had become a source of income and she'd done a little bit of extra work on the side to subsidise any shortfall. She had done some modelling work too during some of the more difficult months but had stuck to only modelling the sort of clothes and products she already wore. So basically jeans and hoodies. Nothing that bared any midriff, or too much skin in general. She tried her best to avoid those sort of jobs but had decided it had to be better than being a runner and getting disillusioned with the industry and lost in the shuffle. The only person's coffee she'd be getting would be her own, she had thought.

The dispenser eventually spluttered into life as coffee mostly poured from the loud machine into the cup below. The machine had definitely seen better days as more unpleasant sounds emulated from it echoing down the empty corridors. Abby grabbed a handful of napkins at the side of the machine and wiped down the spillage from the incompetent dispenser. Why they hadn't replaced this relic like all the other old equipment in the university was anyone's guess.

She scolded the machine, "You've got one job."

The corridor lights began to flicker. One or two at first, then all of them. Abby glanced down the corridor expecting to see a janitor or someone but it was devoid of all life, until she heard a door creak open.

"Hello," she called. There was no answer.

She heard another creak, followed by what could possibly have been a slam. There was normally only a couple of people about when she came here late at night and they were usually quiet like her. Not that slamming a door was a major crime, and probably happened loads during the day, but it was rare during Abby's late night editing sessions. Abby stared a little longer down the hall but no one emerged.

Abby shrugged it off before the lights began to flicker again, then completely switch off. For a brief moment the corridor was plunged into darkness, then the bulbs all pinged back on one by one. Abby shook her head at the old building. However new the equipment and decor might be, it was still an old building she thought to herself. She took her drink from the machine just as loud music blared making her spill the coffee over her hand.

Abby used her free hand to grab the source of the music from her pocket; her mobile. She checked the screen and put it back upon seeing it was Katie who had called. She had no desire to talk to her at that moment, or ever really. Abby's attention turned to the coffee cup, and the coffee that had splashed across her hand.

"Shouldn't you have burnt me?" she enquired. Abby tried the coffee, it didn't even qualify as lukewarm. She looked back towards the coffee machine. "Cold as well, brilliant," she mocked the emotionless inanimate machine.

The lights flickered once more as Abby headed back towards the editing suite and tossed the coffee into a nearby bin. Just like fancy coffees, she didn't do cold coffee either. If it wasn't regular coffee, and didn't burn a little when she drunk it, then it wasn't coffee. She thought she heard another door slam shut and some more creaking but put it down to tiredness, or the old building. Near the editing rooms however she spotted that the door to her suite was open. She swore she closed it. Maybe she hadn't, or maybe this was the source of the creaking and slamming.

As Abby got nearer she heard voices inside the room. She hoped someone had just walked into the wrong room they'd booked, but the flickering lights and door slamming had put her on edge. Plus the coffee machine had pissed her off. So to be on the safe side Abby reached into her bag and placed her hand around the pepper spray she kept there just in case some asshole ever thought it would be a wise idea to attack her while she walked home late one night.

Splatploitation Intrusion

Abby entered the editing suite to find Percy and Roger sitting on the comfy chairs laughing at her short film as it played on the monitor. She didn't recognise who they were at first but was already put out by them being near her work. She also didn't pick up on the laughter being directed at her film, her work was too good for that she had subconsciously thought. Abby did however tighten her grip on the pepper spray seeing as they were in the room without her permission.

"Uh hey," she said without trying to get instantly mad at them for being in her space. She was a guest at the university after all so had to be on her best behaviour and fight her natural instinct not to already be having a go at them. They could just be a couple of older students who had wandered into the wrong room so she didn't want to make an unnecessary scene.

"I'm sorry but this room is already taken." She gestured to the log sheet that hung from the wall to emphasis the statement. It clearly had her name on it and no one else's. "Booked all night," Abby added with a false smile in case they really weren't getting that they shouldn't be here, which seemed to be the case.

Another door slammed down the corridor, this one a lot closer to the room. Abby was the only one who paid attention to it as Percy and Roger were too busy trying to act tough and mysterious.

"We're not here for the editing suite, Ms Jackson," Percy said in an attempted intimidating voice.

"We're here for you," Roger followed with. His voice sounded slightly more intimidating, but still didn't exactly send shivers down Abby's spine. Although she did tighten the grip on the pepper spray once again getting ready to pull it out at a second's notice. She considered turning and running despite not exactly being scared. Clearly these guys had some beef with her, and leaving would be the sensible thing to do, but her curiosity got the better of her.

Yet another door slammed down the corridor. This one sounded extra loud like it came from the editing suite next to them. Percy jumped to his feet and shouted at the doorway.

"For fucksake Matthew! Stop with the door slamming, she's already in here."

At that moment Abby knew who the intruders in front of her were.

"Are you guys the Splatploitation Brothers?" She asked having already figured out the answer.

Percy stood proudly before her. "Indeed we are," he announced while seemingly still trying to keep an air of mystery about them which had undeniably gone.

"What the fuck is wrong with you? You can't just barge in here like this! You're lucky I haven't pepper sprayed the lot of you," Abby ranted at the pair feeling slightly less threatened now she knew who they were.

"We can do what we want," Percy replied like some spoiled brat before she'd even finished. "And what we want to do is talk."

"Then phone. Email. Skype. Zoom. Arrange a meeting. Send a fucking carrier pigeon just don't…" Abby raged before once again being cut off by Percy.

"We don't need to explain ourselves, you do," he said angrily with any sense of perceived coolness now out the window. He'd always been someone quick to anger, especially when it came to his enemies. Although the same could be said about Abby.

Matthew and Duncan pushed into the room forcing Abby to step away from the door and leading to them surrounding her. She kept her hand tightly wrapped around the pepper spray as her other hand slid into her pocket reaching for her phone. It meant she looked rather casual to an outside observer with her hands in her bag and pockets, but she was poised and ready in case the group did anything stupid. She definitely started to feel threatened now though, especially with four of them encircling her, but no way was she going to show it.

While the other three Splatploitation Brothers wore their normal clothes consisting of clever t-shirts and jeans, Matthew had come prepared wearing what was essentially a cat burglar outfit. He thought he'd dressed as a ninja, but everyone else in the room definitely saw it as a cat burglar costume. It had taken a lot of inner monologuing to force himself out of character during a shoot, but his anger towards Abby had overpowered his desire to respect his method. He could drop it just this once if it meant dealing with the lies she was spreading. In a way she probably should have felt honoured that he came out of character for her, but she didn't. She couldn't have cared less. Needless to say despite being surrounded by the group and feeling threatened by the situation as a whole Abby wasn't finding Matthew intimidating in the least. She wanted to laugh at him but was too angry for that at the moment.

"I don't need to explain anything. You guys make horror films, I review them. That's how it works," she told them with an extra edge to her voice.

"No, what we do is create art," Percy countered. Roger turned his nose up at the statement but no one noticed. "What you do is hide behind your blog and trash that art," Percy continued.

Abby considered his statement for a moment. It had been something she'd thought about over the years of writing her blog, especially when she first started. Abby liked to think she was someone who believed any film made was an achievement, and really who was she to judge when she had never made a feature film herself. But she couldn't just review films she loved. She understood the art and believed her own opinion mattered. So whether a film had been good or bad she would state her opinion. Abby had decided from the very beginning of the blog to only ever speak the truth, her truth, and that way it would be fair and consistent. It meant a lot of times she'd maybe come across as rude, but that was part of the business she thought, although she considered it a lot less these days. She had become desensitised to being too harsh in her reviews, which is probably what led to the last Splatploitation Brothers one becoming more personal.

This approach had led to Abby getting a lot of angry emails down the years from both the filmmakers, and the fans of films she'd shat on. She had read all kinds of nasty shit said about her in the emails, and even had some death threats from the more hardcore Splatploitation Brothers fans, but she had always ignored it in the past. Most of the more threatening, disgusting, crude, vile emails she hadn't even finished reading, just sent them straight to the trash folder. The one thing she had never had up until this point however was one of those disgruntled filmmakers approach her in person, let alone four of them at once.

It was this approach which had made Abby not want to back down in the slightest despite it being a precarious situation. If there was one thing she could not tolerate in this world it was a bully. Sure, she had been accused of being one herself plenty with the blog, but this was different. That was critiquing films, this is threatening someone in person. This was in her university, late at night, while she was editing alone. It was four of them surrounding her, trying to intimidate her when they shouldn't even be here. She couldn't abide that, and why should she.

"True," she finally replied to the statement. "But that's

because it is trash. And really… art?" She said with some extra mocking in both her face and voice. She couldn't have sounded more patronising if she tried, which is exactly what she was going for. Fuck them, she thought. How dare they try and strong-arm her like this? It was absolutely unacceptable and she wouldn't stand for it, even if her stomach was feeling sick and her heart was racing at being surrounded.

Once again Roger nodded along to the end of the reply in complete agreement. He didn't believe their films were trash, he was proud of them, but no fucking way did he make art. He was in the entertainment business. He wanted to scare people, or turn them on, or make them puke, or walk out the cinema in utter disgust, or preferably all of the above. What he did not want was to have them care about the use of mise-en-scene or non-diegetic sound. Art was the boring shit he saw on the monitors in front of them, the sort of pretentious bullshit he'd steer well clear of. Roger went to repeat these thoughts out loud but Abby wasn't done so he continued to stand there as the 'muscle.'

"How is anything you've done art? You showed more creativity breaking into the university than anything you've ever put on the screen," Abby barked getting more annoyed as she'd realised they were taking up her precious editing time too. This time it was Matthew who interrupted.

"Your lies about my acting are slanderous and vindictive Miss Jackson," he blurted out already trying his best not to cry.

"I'm entitled to my opinion," Abby fired back, but she wasn't done. "And if you want to change it then take some acting classes and stop with those ridiculous fucking accents!" She said not even being close to finished as she got more and more angry with the group. "And why the fuck are you dressed like a cat burglar, you know all these machines are alarmed right." Abby pointed to the editing equipment like Matthew was planning on stealing it, which he wasn't. "Also there are cameras everywhere," she added to her rant as her head continued to fill with more reasons to be pissed off with them.

"We disabled the cameras," Duncan said with no one paying the slightest bit of attention to him once more.

Matthew's face turned bright red, his nostrils flared, his eyes wide and filled with rage.

"Ridiculous," he shouted loud enough for anyone in the car park across the street to hear. "Utterly ridiculous. Preposterous. The only thing here that's…"

Percy interrupted before Matthew had an aneurysm.

"You will no longer review our films," he said with a sternness to his voice and a look in his eyes, which showed he meant it.

"I'll review whatever I want," Abby replied without hesitation. Her voice was still filled with anger and somehow had shown no signs of breaking. On the inside she was scared, worried, and extremely anxious, but much like her arguments with Katie she had no intention of backing down.

"We'll sue," Duncan interjected a little louder than his previous meek attempt to speak.

Even Abby ignored Duncan and addressed the rest of the group.

"Now if you would all kindly fuck off I have a new post to write about how you guys broke into my editing suite and tried to show off your horror skills by flicking some lights on and off while slamming a couple of doors in fancy dress." She looked at Matthew while shaking her head for the last part with a 'what the fuck are you wearing' expression plastered across on her face.

Percy took a step closer to Abby. Roger stood and followed suit playing his role as the muscle.

"You won't be blogging about us anymore," Percy once

again threatened with extra malice added to his voice.

Abby noted the change in tone. "Are you threatening me?" She asked knowing that he was.

She pulled out her mobile and began to dial. She managed to type one nine when Roger batted the phone from her hand.

"Fucker," she shouted when the phone hit the floor and he aggressively stomped on it.

Abby pulled the pepper spray from her bag before anymore could be said or done. She squirted the whole content of the can into Roger's face as it instantly began to burn. That will teach him.

Abby turned to the door where Matthew blocked her path. She kicked him square between the legs freeing the route before he had even fully realised he was blocking it. His only thoughts after that were whether he was dying or not as he fell to the floor clutching himself in a pain that he had never felt before. He was certain she'd broken something, or that his balls where now tucked up deep inside him. She had kicked him hard, but as always the case with Matthew he was overreacting. That said, it did hurt a lot and he wasn't going to get up anytime soon.

Abby stepped over him as he lay crying on the floor screaming like he had been gunned down. She shoulder-barged Duncan aside who had made a weak attempt to stop her. His heart wasn't in it as he knew she could easily beat him and he wasn't about to take a shot like Matthew. With that she was out of the room before Percy could grab her, not that he was in any kind of rush for a physical confrontation with her either. He had something else in mind.

Magic Camera

Abby hurried down the empty university corridor. There was no point shouting for help, she knew it was unlikely anyone else would be about, not this time of night, plus she didn't want to give the Splatploitation Brothers the satisfaction of thinking they'd scared her. She couldn't believe what had just happened. How dare they attack her? There was no question in her mind that she was going straight to the police, and then would do everything in her power to ruin them. If the last blog had been a bit of a personal attack on them the next one would be all out fucking war. She wasn't a vindictive person, but they had massively crossed a line. She was flabbergasted. Creeps.

It was times like this Abby wished landlines were still a thing. She had often teased her mum about using such relics having fully grown up on mobile phones, but now she'd give anything to see one after that oaf crushed her mobile. She just wanted to call the police and have them all immediately arrested. Her mind started wandering to all the information on her phone. That phone was her life in a lot of ways. Luckily all the script notes and ideas she had written within the phone were backed up elsewhere but Abby was already thinking what a hassle sorting out a new phone was going to be. It was like a mini production studio for her, with most of her career, and work, documented on it. The only saving grace was it had been crushed not stolen. At least they couldn't invade her privacy like they had her editing suite. Abby shuddered at the thought.

She glanced back to see Percy emerging from the editing room clutching something in his hand which looked like a gun. Abby's heart stopped for a brief millisecond before she realised it wasn't quite the right shape and size to be a gun. Percy didn't attempt to give chase, just stood in the doorway with an excited grin on his face. Abby stopped when she was far enough down the long corridor to look at the object once again in his hand despite everything in her brain begging her to flee. Once again curiosity got the better of her. She was momentarily relieved when she worked out it definitely wasn't a gun, but why on Earth was he holding an old Super 8 camera?

The camera had a black square body with a silver lens and a long handle at the bottom which Percy was holding. A couple of dials were stuck to the side along with an exposure meter and a wrist strap that Percy wasn't using. The camera had some scratches down the right-hand side and the handle had a slight dent from when Percy had dropped it once, but Abby didn't know or see any of that. She just saw the basic shape and lens and, much to her relief, the fact that it wasn't actually a gun.

Abby had used one of these cameras herself briefly during her classes but this camera wasn't from the university. It didn't have the black 'property of' sticker which was stuck to all the equipment in the uni. The similar camera Abby had used was in a film history class in which they learnt about different film cameras and negatives from the past. None of the class, including Abby, had shown any real interest in the camera or the history of them.

She liked old movies, maybe even more than modern movies, but she wasn't interested in the equipment from the past. She didn't have a darkroom or anything to splice negatives with, and it all looked like it took far too long. Sure she loved the look of film stock and was disappointed with the fact that it's a dying breed, but in her mind it had had its time. She would never have been able to make her short film the old way, it would have been far too expensive and more difficult than necessary.

Everyone in the class had felt the same. That the old process was just too time consuming and well, past it. They looked at the old cameras wondering how on earth anyone got anything done when they could now do the exact same thing with a click of a button on their phones. The professor had valiantly tried to explain that it wasn't the same thing, but he couldn't get through to the students. Even Abby looked bored and she normally wanted to learn everything about movies. She just wasn't interested in old tools of the when they didn't help her in the here and now. Seeing the images of old movies could help her, but how they were taken was of no use in her eyes.

Percy slowly lifted the ancient looking camera in Abby's direction until he was aiming it straight at her. The other Splatploitation Brothers joined him in the hallway as Abby stood looking somewhat dumbfounded at the camera, wondering what the fuck was going on. An idea caught in her mind.

"Are you filming this?" She angrily asked. "Is this some kind of sick game to you?"

They didn't answer.

Abby once again couldn't believe they had done this. Breaking into her editing suite and threatening her was bad enough, but were they doing it as part of a film they were making? Was this meant to be one of those found footage type movies? It wasn't the sort of thing they'd made before, but it had started to feel like they were having a go. Did they think threatening her would get a genuine reaction? Sick fucks. What if she had pulled a knife or gun from her bag instead of pepper spray? What would they have done then?

Abby knew she should carry on running, but she wanted answers. She waited on them for a reply but there still wasn't one. Had they been filming her this whole time? Is that what all the light flicking and door slamming had been about earlier? She hadn't seen them up until the point where they had broken into her editing suite, but now her skin was crawling with the thought that they could have had been spying on her all evening. How long had those twisted fucks been watching her?

She continued to stare down the hallway. Roger used a water bottle to help try and get his vision back while doing his best not to rub his eyes. His whole face still felt like it was on fire. Matthew had dragged himself to the doorway while still on the floor holding where his balls used to be and looking at Abby with pure hatred pouring from him in-between his exaggerated cries. Duncan stood behind the others barely in sight while Percy remained eerily calm. He just stood there with a menacing grin on his face and the Super 8 camera stretched out in his hand.

Then he finally spoke.

"Time for you to be our new muse," Percy broadcast barely able to contain his delight.

"I fucking knew it," Abby both thought and said taking this as confirmation that she was right, and these sick fucks were using her to make some dodgy movie. She hadn't seen any of them with a camera in the editing suite, but as she pointed out there were security cameras everywhere and Duncan had bragged about hacking into them. Or was that disarming them? Either way now she knew what they were doing she wanted to ruin them even more. If there was one thing worse than watching a fucking Splatploitation Brothers film it had to be being in one see thought while absolutely seething.

Trouble was she had guessed wrong.

The motor in the Super 8 camera began to click into motion. A loud whirring sound poured out of the camera like it hadn't been used in decades. That was certainly a possibility considering how old the camera was, but it wasn't that. Abby continued her confused stare while Percy began a maniacal laugh. Abby had no fucking clue what was so funny, but soon the rest of the group had joined in with his laughter. Apparently they were all in on whatever the joke was.

And that's when it happened.

Abby didn't really know what was happening at first. It was just a light rumble in the air when it began - a vibration of sorts. Then the walls began to move, at least that's what she thought. But it wasn't movement as such, more like a flicker. A really jerky flicker. She could hear the clicking of the camera growing louder but she couldn't see the camera anymore, or the Splatploitation Brothers.

Ahead of her was a bright white light. Not the sort you're meant to see when you die, more like the room was massively overexposed. The clicking didn't make any sense either. It was like a roll of film going through the camera but it was too loud. Way too loud in fact. She should never have been able to hear it from where she was, at least not at such a volume.

"What is…" she began to ask before her attention turned back to the corridor walls. The flickering had momentarily stopped, but now the colours of the corridor were changing. They began to saturate and bleed into each other while the lights above her washed out just like the end of the corridor. She thought she could hear the faint sounds of the Splatploitation Brothers still laughing but it could have easily been in her head. Whatever this all was it didn't feel like a found footage movie being shoot without her permission anymore. Something far more sinister and fucking weird was happening.

Had they drugged her, Abby thought. Maybe that's what had happened with the coffee machine and why the coffee was cold. She shook the thought from her head the moment it formed. The coffee was often cold here, it was an old shitty machine. But they had done something because she definitely felt like she was tripping. She thought she saw large thick black dots on the walls as they washed out too but put it down to her eyes playing tricks. Like when you wake up staring out of the window to sunshine that's too bright.

Abby shielded her eyes as she tried to look back towards the editing suite, but the light was blinding. Or was it? It felt to Abby more like there wasn't anything there anymore. That the whiteness wasn't a light, it was just nothing. Not an empty space as such, more a wall of nothing. Either way, neither the Splatploitation Brothers, nor anything else appeared to be there anymore. The loud clicking of the camera had started to fade. Abby could still hear it, but it lacked the menacing pulsating beat it had moments earlier. Now it sounded like it was winding down rather than cranking up.

She'd had enough of this. Abby had to get out of there. She turned to run, but as she stepped forward there was no ground beneath her anymore. Instead she fell. At first she descended into blackness, a deep dark well devoid of anything. The rumbling had stopped too, along with the vibrations. Now there wasn't any sound at all as even the light clicking of the old camera had come to a halt. There was just complete blackness and perfect quiet. It didn't last long as she landed hard on something solid and with an overly loud thud. She wasn't sure what she had landed on and didn't have time to work it out as whatever the ground was it knocked her clean out on impact.

Abby lay completely unconscious in a pit of darkness unaware what had happened to her or where she now was.

The Pit

Abby awoke unaware how long she'd been out cold or where the hell she was. The one thing she did instantly know was she wasn't wearing the same clothes anymore. Instead of her normal comfy hoodie and jeans she was wearing a pair of blue cut-off denim shorts and a flimsy black vest top. It was simply not Abby at all and much too revealing for her taste. Her exposed legs alone were enough to send her into some kind of anxiety spiral, but this wasn't the time for that.

Her hands squished in the mud beneath her. The ground as a whole was hard, but it had a layer of softness on the top that had failed to ease the impact of the fall but had succeeded in getting her a little dirty. Abby pushed herself upwards and staggered to her feet. Now a little less groggy and more upright, she looked to her skimpy clothes once more with the shorts already looking muddy.

"What the fuck!" She looked around for her normal clothes but they weren't there. Nothing was there except for mud. She was alone, in some kind of ditch, wearing clothes that showed far too much of her body.

She looked straight up. It was a tall ditch, maybe three times the height of her. Luckily there was a ridiculously big bright moon so the ditch was well lit otherwise Abby may have thought she was buried underground. A couple of lone stars shone in the sky, and the night air was warm, but everything was overshadowed by the outwardly unrealistic moon. A howling in the distance broke her concentration.

Abby squinted her eyes trying to see if the Splatploitation Brothers were looking down on her. She couldn't see them or hear their voices but suspected they had to be there.

"What the hell do you guys think you're doing?" She

shouted trying to mask the fear in her voice. She didn't do a great job of hiding it. But then she was stuck in a ditch in some unknown place, alone and scared with the distinct possibility looming over her that she may soon be buried alive. Abby had held it together in the editing suite and even the university corridor, but this was too much. She looked at her clothes once more focusing on them as the current source of her anger.

"You are so all going to jail for this," she said sounding more like her normal self, but her fear was quickly rising

Abby continued to stare upwards trying to remember what exactly happened. She remembered being at the university working on her short film before the Splatploitation Brothers had invaded her editing suite. She had escaped the room and ran but then stopped when Percy pointed a gun at her. No it wasn't a gun she remembered, it was a camera. And then… well, then it got fuzzy. What she thought she remembered couldn't possibly be true. She felt her forehead. The hard landing had left a small lump but nothing life threatening.

Why the fuck did she stop? She had got away but then froze when she looked back and saw the not gun in Percy's hand. From that moment onwards everything felt wrong, she remembered that part. It all felt very, very wrong, confusing even. She had stopped because she wanted answers but now had nothing but questions.

She tried to remember more but couldn't, or at least didn't trust the memory. She had thought they were shooting a film but remembered that was her theory, not a fact. More important she remembered nothing which would remotely explain why the fuck she was wearing different clothes. When did that happen? Where had they taken her? Abby examined the sides of the ditch, mud and rock all the way up. She sunk her fingers into the soft mud of the ditch wall and began to heave herself upwards. Mostly to escape the ditch but also to take her mind off why she was in different clothes.

Abby was a good climber and always had been. Her father used to take her hill walking and sometimes they'd climb up the side of cliffs. To Abby climbing was as easy as riding a bike, although she couldn't actually ride a bike. She skipped that part to learn to climb, which currently felt like the correct decision. She'd stopped climbing with her dad when she was around fifteen acting like it was an embarrassment.

It was silly really. She enjoyed it and loved having something that was just theirs. But she was fifteen and spending time climbing with her dad was frowned upon within the social circles of school. It wasn't long after this when she ditched caring about those sort of things and began to fully embrace her more loner lifestyle, but she didn't go back to climbing. She wished she had. Maybe she'd correct that next time she saw her folks.

Abby spotted a rock halfway up the wall and clawed her fingers around it. She began to drag herself upwards with the support of the rock until it began to tilt forward. The tilt forward revealed that it wasn't actually a rock at all. Abby had her fingers stuck in the eye socket of a human skull. The brittle skull shattered in her hand as she put too much pressure on it. The break sent Abby crashing back to the hard dirt with the ruptured skull landing beside her.

"Ouch," she said, holding her side after the awkward landing.

Before she had time to investigate her side further or even be freaked out by the human skull laying in pieces next to her, a grotty rotten hand exploded from the ground beneath her. It shattered the last remains of the skull as it made a grab for Abby. She instinctively rolled to the side of the ditch avoiding the outstretched hand that tried to snatch her. Another hand reached from beneath the mud, then a third. Abby jumped to her feet despite being in shock at the ambush and stamped down hard on the first hand breaking its rotten wrist with ease.

The hands were all human hands but not alive human hands. They were green and rotten with most of the skin missing and a lot of bone showing. They looked like they were three-quarters of the way though decomposing and some seemed mutated as well. One of the hands had two fingers missing and another had a thumb in the wrong place. It was in between two of the fingers instead. The remaining rotting skin was falling from the hands as they flailed around trying to grab Abby creating a most disgusting carpet in an already grim muddy ditch.

Abby stood on the broken hand again as it retreated back into the ground. She followed it up with a stomp on the second hand sending it into retreat in a macabre version of Whack-a-Mole. Several more hands penetrated the surface as Abby leapt to the muddy wall to avoid them. She clung on to the side of the wall with her fingers firmly dug in. Not for the first time that evening she wondered what the fuck was going on.

The decomposed hands below her continued their search as they grabbed at the space Abby used to occupy. They desperately searched while Abby watched from a few feet above them. She wasn't exactly sure what they would do if they got hold of her but was in no mood to find out. And why the fuck were there decaying hands sticking out the ground trying to attack her anyway? She wanted to reach for her head certain that she must have bumped it harder than she thought but it wasn't worth the risk of falling. For the moment she'd just have to accept what was in front of her eyes no matter how wildly unrealistic and stupid it felt.

Abby studied the hands for a few more moments trying to work out what exactly they were but she wasn't any closer to an answer. Sure, she'd seen this in films plenty of times, but this was real life, and in real life hands didn't explode from the fucking ground. But then in the real world she didn't wear short shorts either so who knew what the rules were anymore.

One of the hands broke free of the muddy surface and immediately began to climb towards Abby. Now it had broken clear of the dirt she saw it was a whole arm, and not just a hand. So now she was being chased up a tall ditch by a severed skeleton arm that was shedding the last remains of its decomposed skin. They really must have drugged her, Abby thought.

Abby reached upwards and pulled herself further away from the disgusting arm that was slowly climbing towards her. The other hands had remained below encased in their muddy prison aimlessly grabbing at the space in which Abby used to be, but this one seemed more focused on her. More determined if that was possible. As far as she could tell it didn't have eyes, but then why would it? It's an arm so it must have been able to just sense her. She had kept still when it first came for her so it wasn't movement it tracked, it just knew. As it drew nearer Abby kicked out at the dead arm but its rotten hand grabbed her ankle sending more flakes of skin from the arm gently floating to the pit below.

It tried to pull Abby down towards the other hands but Abby held on tight to the side of the wall. She dragged herself higher, closer to the top of the ditch. More hands burst from the ground below her. They cracked through the surface with ease but none of them were able to escape their dirt prison unlike the one currently holding on tightly to Abby's ankle. They all had to just wait patiently below hoping she was tossed down to them.

Abby tried shaking off the dead hand but it had a firm grip. It wasn't a grip that hurt her in any way, but she could feel that the hand had a bit of force behind it. She slammed her leg against the side of the ditch with the arm in between hoping to either hurt it or for it to let go and fall back to the bottom of the pit. It did neither. Instead the rogue dead arm kept hold of her. It wasn't going to be shaken off that easily. It was definitely tougher than the ones she had stomped on.

She climbed a little higher and was almost within arm's reach of the top of the ditch. The severed arm unsuccessfully continued to try and pull her down to the rest of its skeleton hand friends beneath them. Looking from afar it would have looked like Abby had a skeleton arm just dangling from her leg, but it wasn't just dangling, it really was somehow pulling her. She could feel it trying, like a toddler trying to get attention. Except this wasn't some little rug rat but instead was a severed skeleton arm with some kind of nefarious agenda.

Abby stretched her arm out and grabbed the top of the ditch. With a somewhat desperate heave she pulled herself upwards and much to her relief broke free of the deep pit. The relief didn't last long as Abby caught sight of her next question the moment she broke free. Also she still had the immediate problem of the dead arm dangling from her leg that was unperturbed by her escape.

Skeletons

At the top of the ditch Abby starred directly at a wooden cross that marked the spot she'd just clawed out of. Several items hung from the cross that included animal teeth, feathers, and chunks of human flesh. The teeth looked like they might have been pulled from a wild cat while the feathers looked like something someone thought a Native American might wear. The flesh was diced into cubes and threaded together to form some kind of morbid necklace. It could have just as easily been chunks of lamb, but Abby knew it was human, or at least it seemed like that was what it was meant to be. None of it made any sense whatsoever but then to Abby neither did the corpse arm still hanging from her ankle.

She heaved herself fully out of the ill-fated pit and closer to the cross. Now within an arm's length she spotted a bunch of twigs tightly strung together and shaped like a person also sitting by the other cursed looking objects. More worrying still was the words she could now see angrily inscribed on to the wooden cross. 'Abby Jackson.' She inched away from the open grave trying not to let the inscription bother her, but quite frankly it was fucking freaky and she began to seriously lose her shit. A glimpse of a question entered her mind further exacerbating matters. It was only brief but enough to freak her out even more. Was she dead?

Is that what had happened in the corridor at the university? Was it actually a gun? Could Percy have shot and killed her? Is that what death felt like? The lights changing, the colours draining, the sound droning before a pit of darkness swallowed her whole. Metaphorically it made sense, but death wasn't the sensation she felt at the time. It didn't feel, for lack of a better word, right. Of course she was no expert but it all just felt too trippy to be death. She imagined death to be more final and absolute than that, more clinical perhaps. Plus if this was hell, why the fuck was she here? Yeah she'd been rude plenty of times, and maybe hurt some people's feelings, and had most certainly never been near a fucking church, but surely that wasn't enough to be down below with the literal monsters.

She simply couldn't be dead, her life had barely started. It wouldn't be fair. She hadn't travelled the world yet or won an Oscar. Fuck she hadn't even kissed the pizza dude. She wondered why that was on her brief bucket list, but it was. She wanted to make at least ten feature films, attend premieres, maybe even mingle with the stars. She didn't like socialising but figured she could handle that. No, death was not an option. This had to be something else, anything else.

"What the fuck is going on?" She shouted out to anyone and everyone. But nobody was around, at least nobody living it seemed.

The severed arm had worked its way up from Abby's ankle while she wasn't paying attention. It had crawled along her leg, past her thigh and onto her stomach as she had stood contemplating the possibility of her demise. The graveyard setting certainly didn't help her line of thinking. Abby noticed her cross wasn't the only one here. She was standing in the middle of a whole host of other crosses stretching in every direction. All had writing on them as well. In fact they all had the exact same thing harshly whittled onto them. 'Abby Jackson.'

The decaying skeleton arm took its opportunity while Abby stared open-mouthed at the graves. It leapt from her chest and grabbed her neck. Boney fingers clawed around her throat and began to squeeze. Its grip wasn't immediately life threatening but it was certainly highly disconcerting and sent Abby into a panic as she suddenly remembered the dead arms existence. If

she'd had time to think about it she would have scolded herself
for forgetting about the arm, even though crawling out of your
own grave is probably a pretty good excuse for any lapses in
concentration. But she didn't have time to think. She just had to
get the fucking thing off her.

Abby reached for the arm trying to yank it from her throat
but couldn't get a good grip. It kept flapping around in an
unnatural pattern. Every time Abby thought she had a good
hold on it her fingers slipped away. It was clearly aware of what
she was trying to do. She could feel its fingers tightening. The
pressure on her throat increasing. No doubt about it, the ultra-
creepy disgusting thing wanted to kill her. She tried to calm
herself but her panic was increasing.

Yet another thought entered Abby's mind that she wished
hadn't. Was this somehow her own arm? It had come out of a
grave marked with her name. But then, so had Abby herself. The
thoughts were far too existential to deal with now, but still…
was it her arm? First things first, she had to get that fucking arm,
whoever's it was, off her throat and fast. She managed to calm
herself for a moment and focus on the arm. Not just flail her
own hands at it, but actually focus. Her eyes followed the arms
movements getting a sense of what it was doing and then she
made her move. Abby snapped her arm forward with surprising
speed. Finally she grabbed it. Bingo.

Gripped with both hands now Abby tugged at the rank arm.
She could feel the bony fingers trying to tighten their grip,
desperate to stay attached to her exposed throat, but they were
slipping away. A finger came loose as the pressure around
Abby's throat released and she was able to swallow the breath
that had been building inside her. The desperation she had been
feeling began to dissipate as her breathing returned to
something closer to normal.

Another finger slipped from her throat and suddenly Abby

regained control. She yanked with all her might and the arm lost its hold. It dangled from Abby's hand like a wild animal being held within arm's length from its tail. She had seen the scene many times in wildlife documentaries of snakes being held in this way but never thought she'd recreate it with a dead arm that might possibly somehow inexplicably be her own.

Without thinking any further Abby slammed the captured arm over her creepy wooden grave. The arm smashed against the wood cracking the right side of the cross and dislodging the interconnecting bones of the arm. The feathers and morbid flesh necklace fell to the floor alongside the twig voodoo doll thing. She raised what remained of the dead arm high in the air again and brought it down harder this time destroying what was left of the cross and breaking the arm in two.

She tossed the upper part of the broken arm into the pit. The hand briefly lay on the floor still able to move as it tried to get off the back of the hand like a turtle lying on its shell. Abby didn't give it the chance as she booted it into the ditch as well. She kicked the doll, necklace, and feathers into the pit for good measure too. Fuck all of them. The teeth remained but only because Abby hadn't noticed them otherwise they'd have suffered the same fate.

What the fuck had just happened was her only thought as the hand hit the bottom of the ditch. How was any of that even remotely possible? Was she dreaming? Her mind once again returned to the notion of being drugged, which had become a far better option than being dead. Whatever they had used was powerful shit as that felt all too real. She could feel the pressure around her neck and the lack of oxygen reaching her brain as that thing tried to strangle her to death.

Abby looked around properly for the first time. She was definitely in some kind of graveyard, but it didn't look or feel right at all. For starters all the wooden crosses had her name on them and looked exactly the same. Like Ikea had mass-produced her headstone. Secondly all the graves looked freshly filled. She hadn't noticed that earlier, but now she could see they weren't open like hers. Dirt protruded from the ground in front of each cross like they had all only just been buried. All the dirt in front of each grave was the same height, width, and consistency too. Abby wasn't sure why she noticed that, but she did. It was just kind of obvious when she was really looking at all of them together.

The graveyard was surrounded by tall trees on every side of it. The trees looked menacing in the night sky despite the bright moon giving them some texture. The branches all looked sharp and stuck out from every conceivable angle. The leaves on the trees were sparse, almost like there shouldn't be any, but not in the 'it's autumn and the leaves have fallen' way. These trees felt like they wanted to show off their dangerous jagged branches and the leaves would somehow inconvenience that.

There was no path within the graveyard either. Nor were there any markers or indication of where she was within the cemetery itself. Abby couldn't see a gate or any fencing from her viewpoint. It truly looked like she was just in the middle of a mysterious graveyard within some creepy dangerous looking woods. Little did she know that's exactly where she was. Even the impossibly bright moon couldn't make this place feel less creepy. Not that graveyards aren't always creepy, but this one felt like it was going out of its way to be extra sinister. Abby wished she had some clue where she was, some kind of sign or hint that gave the game away a little, but there was nothing.

She'd settle for something that could inform her that she at least wasn't dead having just crawled out of her own grave, but no such reassurances were around. She tried to put it to the back of her mind for the moment, tried to calm herself from the thoughts that her life was over. Part of her knew this couldn't be the end. That it didn't feel like death despite the open grave with her name on it and the impossibility of the skeleton arm attack. But another part of her did think it was possible and she simply didn't want to fully address it at this time. She decided to listen to the part of her which thought she wasn't dead. But if she wasn't dead and in some kind of hell, then where the fuck was she?

It was difficult to work out what direction she should head from this point. It all looked exactly the same. Abby heard another howl in the distance which sounded like it came from her left but she couldn't be sure. Without any other indication of where to go Abby decided left wasn't the way. She'd already dealt with a severed decomposing skeleton arm that tried to choke her to death, she wasn't in the mood for wolves, or whatever made that sound.

So Abby decided out of the three remaining options straight on was the best bet. She liked to believe she was someone in life who always went forward no matter the challenges, so why not take on that belief now, even if maybe she wasn't in life anymore. As she took her first step forward another arm exploded from the ground. This one however wasn't just an arm, as a head began to emerge with it.

Zombies

Abby booted the fucking head clean off before it had even fully emerged from the ground beneath her. In fact, it was even before she could have fully known the head was attached to something and not just running around like the arm she had just dispatched. The head emerging from the ground had spooked her and Abby had kicked out to protect herself. The next thing she saw was the decapitated head sailing off into the distance. She didn't even think she kicked it that hard, but it flew a fair old way. It landed in the woods Abby was about to head towards, which definitely gave her second thoughts about going that direction.

She had watched it fly from the deck after losing her balance on the follow through still expecting the to be a head there. The arms and the rest of the body had gone limp when the head was removed. This didn't feel like the skeleton arm she had battled with moments earlier, this was something new. On closer inspection of the headless corpse she knew straight away what she was dealing with. The thought would have been impossible hours ago, but there was no mistaking it. She'd just been attacked by a zombie. Or rather she had just attacked a zombie as in theory she hit him first. All he'd really done was spook her, but he won't be doing that again.

Two more zombies burst from the ground as Abby helplessly sat staring at the decapitated stiff. Their hands grabbed at any part of her body they could get a hold on. The first zombie gripped her ankle once more while also wrapping itself round her right leg. The other zombie came from behind grabbing her forehead and putting its other grubby decomposing worm ridden mitt across her tits. That was the hand she seized first.

She swore it copped a feel but this wasn't the time to be

bringing it up on sexual harassment charges. A more vigilante approach was required. She ripped the arm right off the zombies fucking shoulder like it was nothing. Abby then kicked the head off the zombie that lay across the ground holding her ankle before swatting aside the remaining arm of the pervert zombie from her forehead before either could cause any damage.

Unlike the skeleton arms these zombies still had some meat to them. Abby didn't get a great look as she'd blindly grabbed it, nevertheless she could still feel its muscle and skin. It was decomposing like the skeleton arm, just at a much earlier stage. Their clothes were dirty and dusty but in a dry manner despite coming from the ground beneath her. Again it didn't feel right. Far too many things hadn't felt right in Abby's eyes, which was understandable when dealing with skeleton arms, open graves, and now fucking zombies all in the middle of an unknown cemetery.

Abby leapt to her feet and curb stomped the perverted zombie back into the dirt cracking his decaying head into two. That will teach him, she thought before screaming out once again.

"Seriously, what the fuck is going on?" Still no one answered. Not that she was expecting them to, but this felt like a moment when someone should have shouted cut or intervened. She'd seen so many movies with this exact scenario. How could any of this actually be real?

From the tree line she saw a horde of zombies emerge. There must have been fifteen to twenty in total. They were a little too far away to tell exactly, and she wasn't about to stand there and count. Either way there were definitely enough to worry her. Abby spun ready to head in a different direction but another three zombies blocked the route as they ambled forward in their incredibly slow manner. She'd always preferred the slow moving zombies of the Romero films to those new high speed athletic zombies of the modern era, but never more so than now. They really were painstakingly slow and Abby felt in no real danger of being caught, although was obviously still annoyed at being stalked by zombies.

Abby had always had mixed feeling about zombie flicks. Like many a film student she enjoyed the social and political commentary of the original Romero films, and some of the ones that followed, but lately she had been 'zombied' out. She preferred haunting supernatural horrors and stuff which played on the mind, rather than things that just wanted to eat your flesh. She knew zombies had their place in the horror world and would still watch them, but they just felt kind of lame to her.

Having now seen one up close she hadn't changed her mind. Sure, they were intimidating because they were the walking dead, but that's all they really had going for them. They lacked the class of the classic Universal monsters, or the menace of other creatures of the night. They just kind of pathetically drooped along looking sad and ready to fall apart at any moment. Abby wasn't impressed. She wasn't about to tell them that they were lame, but after the evening she'd had Abby felt she could safely handle a zombie or two. Just probably not a whole horde.

Their speed and bad posture weren't the only things Abby noticed as the three zombies slowly stalked towards her. The zombies all looked the same. Not similar, but exactly the same. It was the same bland looking dead person, times three. She looked to the decapitated head of the zombie who had grabbed her legs and noticed he looked identical to the three approaching her. The perverted zombie looked alike as well even with his face spilt in two and half-buried in the ground. Abby noticed a creepy smile on its ruptured face. She stamped on his head again breaking it into more pieces knowing exactly what that smile had been about. Fucking creeper.

If they had come from the graves in the cemetery then why were all the headstones marked 'Abby Jackson' because these nondescript zombies were guys and looked nothing like her, not even at a fleeting glance. Had the first one she fought looked the same as these? She couldn't picture his face in her mind mostly because she had dropkicked him out of the graveyard before he'd even emerged. Either way five looking exactly the same was already fucking weird, what would one more change.

Out of the four possible directions Abby could go one was blocked off by three slow moving zombies and another was guarded by an even slower approaching horde. The final two options consisted of a possible wolf, wolf pack, or werewolf considering how the rest of the night had gone, and a decapitated zombie head that hopefully was now dead dead. Out of the four possibilities a zombie head lying around in the dirt somewhere seemed undoubtably the best choice whether it was dead dead or not.

Abby started making her way in the direction of the zombie head as the ground beneath her kept rumbling. Every few steps another zombie emerged from its dirt grave trying to snatch her. Now that she was expecting it Abby easily avoided each attempt and carried on forward. The one which had escaped the ground and managed to sneak up on her, she punched in the face and kicked backwards.

He fell perfectly onto one of the crosses which penetrated his body in one smooth slick motion. The zombie didn't (for a lack of better word) die though, it just struggled while pinned to the wooden cross. He looked rather pathetic flapping his arms around trying to escape, but Abby wasn't in the mood to laugh. She did notice however that the pinned zombie also looked like the ones approaching her so decided that all the zombies in the graveyard did look exactly the same. All boring as fuck looking like they should have been working in a post office if it wasn't for them being the undead.

The three behind her had increased in numbers as some fully escaped the ground, but they were nearly out of sight and even less of a threat. The horde to her right hadn't seemed to have moved from their original starting position, they were that slow. Another loud howl emanated from the other direction that sounded much closer than the previous times and reinforced Abby's decision to carry on going straight ahead.

Had she been sitting at home watching this unfold on a TV she would have undoubtedly been screaming at the screen it was a trap. That she was being lead somewhere. Here in the moment though, it hadn't crossed her mind. She knew what the other options held and didn't like any of them, so the unknown felt safer. The lesser of all the evils.

Abby could see the tree line clearer as she neared it. From closer up it looked even more sinister than before. The branches were stripped of any natural life and the end of each were razor sharp. She spotted a slight opening to the left of her but it looked a tight squeeze. She knew she could probably tackle the zombies behind her and look for another possible way out of the graveyard but didn't like the unknown entity of the close-sounding howls. Plus it wasn't three zombies anymore with several more having joined them creating the beginnings of a second horde.

Although the zombies had been easy enough to deal with, there did seem to be an endless supply of them, and that skeleton hand had also nearly caused some serious damage. Abby didn't like the look of these trees one bit and was sure she'd get a few pricks from them, but she'd thoroughly had enough of this graveyard and its inhabitants. She just wanted out.

Abby rushed to the opening readying to enter. She had a glance to the left and right of the woods before poking her head carefully inside. The trees and branches just looked dead to her. The few leaves which were about were making their way from being a dirty brown to an ominous black. Whatever this forest was it was dead now, which may explain the walking dead behind her. It didn't matter either way. Abby had made her mind up and this was the only way she could go.

She stepped through the narrow opening into the dead forest not noticing the tree branch slowly slithering beside her...

Entangled

The forest was a lot darker than Abby had first realised as even the excessively bright moon failed to fully penetrate the trees. The branches had formed a canopy entangling with each other to give the forest a creepy roof that shielded it from the moon and the outside world in general. No leaves were required for the canopy which was just as well for the woods as there weren't many. Just a lot of evil-looking branches. A few slivers of moonlight had battled through. Enough to maybe see a couple of feet in front, and add an odd pool of light here and there, but that was it. Other than that, near darkness.

Abby walked slowly and carefully inside the dark forest and soon found herself having to crouch. The branches had bunched together tighter and tighter lowering the self-made roof of the forest and forcing Abby onto her knees. While a bit awkward, it had to be better than the presumably brain eating alternative she had left behind. Abby was getting the odd jab to her side from the branches but crawled at a slow enough speed not to get hurt. Again, the odd branch prod to her side was probably better than the odd zombie bite to her face.

It really was a tangled mess inside the forest. It was impossible to tell what branches belonged to what trees. However they barely looked like trees, just dead wood sticking from the ground and poking out in all directions. Luckily there seemed to be a path of sorts leading Abby through the beginnings of the forest because if she had to guide herself she would have definitely got lost with the poor light. As it was there was just a single way to go, any other direction you'd end up impaled on a tree.

One of the branches snagged Abby's face lightly scratching her. As she move slightly to the side away from the harmful branch another scraped her arm. Neither scratch was life threatening, or even anything more than cosmetic, but both were a reminder of the dangers of the forest and for Abby to remain vigilant. She kept moving forward determined to make it through to whatever awaited on the other side. Abby wasn't sure where the forest lead, or how long it would take to get through, but she knew these scratches were better than dealing with skeleton arms and zombies… until she caught a glimpse of a branch moving alongside her.

She put it down to her imagination at first. After all she had landed hard in a ditch, possibly been drugged, and had been attacked numerous times by things that simply couldn't exist. But then she saw it move again. It wasn't a big movement, nothing *Evil Dead* style. No sweeping forward or swooping down at her. Just a little movement. It could have been the wind with how lightly it moved, but this wasn't a caught in the breeze type of movement. This was more like a slithering snake.

Abby quickly put the thought out of her mind. Not much scared her, neither in horror films or real life, but she couldn't handle snakes. She wasn't even sure why. It wasn't like she'd ever had a bad experience with a snake, but they creeped her the fuck out. The way they looked, the way they moved, the hissing sound, the texture, probably the smell if she had any idea what they smelt like. She just did not like snakes one little bit. But this wasn't a snake, just a branch that seemed to move of its own accord. Much better, she sarcastically reasoned.

The trees grew tighter together as Abby crawled further into the woods. Barely any of the moonlight now managed to break through the impenetrable barrier that was the forest canopy. Whatever the reason for the moon being impossibly massive and ridiculously bright, it wasn't enough. It had no power or dominance here. The forest just grew darker at a time when Abby needed it to get lighter.

With the tightness and the darkness came the inevitable feeling of claustrophobia. Abby wasn't someone who considered herself claustrophobic and hadn't even thought about it while in the dark dank pit, but this was different. The absence of the sky unnerved Abby and that was before the possibly moving branch. In the pit no matter how narrow and unsettling it was she could see the sky. She knew she was a good climber and could get out. There was some comfort to that, even in the scary situation.

But this forest had no end in sight. No glimmer of comfort. Abby could barely see her hands in front of her face. Climbing counted for nothing in these woods either as these weren't the sort of trees you could climb. They were barely trees at all. Plus she couldn't even stand let alone climb with that low sinister-looking canopy roof. If light couldn't even get through the roof there was no way Abby could. The tiny pools of light that could somehow still pierce the canopy had grown dimmer. They had faded into the mud beneath her leaving the small rays of light as a possible progress marker rather than something to warn her of any dangers ahead.

Abby crawled forward a few more paces before she caught a slight glimpse of movement again. The branch had followed her, there was no doubt about it. It didn't matter that she couldn't clearly see it, it had definitely followed her. Her gut backed the feeling up, and if there was one thing Abby always trusted, it was her gut. It was always ahead of her brain. Unfortunately, movement or not, there wasn't too much she could do about it at that precise time.

She tried to keep an eye on the branch but it just led to her not paying full attention to the trees in front of her. Several different branches poked Abby in quick succession. Each one made her jump and land on another like some kind of sadistic pinball machine. Thanks to the skimpy clothes she had somehow ended up wearing Abby could instantly see the bruises form on her arms and legs and wanted to again curse the outfit change.

She was one hundred percent positive her normal jeans and hoodie would have offered a lot more protection. Her mind briefly went back to horror thoughts of how she ended up in these clothes, but she couldn't allow herself to think about that at the moment. That was a big fucking battle for another time and someone was definitely going to pay for it. She knew the only way through this current situation would be to stay calm. Easier said than done.

"What kind of fucking forest is this?" She muttered under her breath trying to refocus herself.

The branch began to crawl in her direction at a much quicker rate than before. It wasn't lighting fast, but it didn't feel to Abby like the branch was hiding itself anymore. Maybe it had overheard the insult. Suddenly the branch whipped forward lashing out at Abby. Luckily she had regained her focus in time and had kept a watchful eye on the rogue branch. She managed to duck her head and avoid the wicked lash that would have slapped her right in the face.

Great, she thought, another thing which probably wanted to attack and kill her. It had become the theme of the evening from the university onwards, assuming she was still on the same day. Who knew anymore? The rules for what was possible and impossible had been tossed aside since she had landed in that grave. No, she thought, before that. What the fuck had happened in that corridor? Unfortunately now wasn't the time to contemplate that question, and she didn't have the answer anyway. She really did need to stop her mind wandering and get the fuck out of this miserable forest.

Abby sped up her crawl taking a lot more chances than she'd like to now the possibility of being whipped in the face or killed by an evil tree branch was a thing. The whole forest felt like a maze, but fortunately a maze with a single path. Abby's greatest fear, other than snakes, was the possibility that any second the path was going to diverge into several others. So far it hadn't, but nevertheless the thought it could was now stuck in her head. The branch trailed just behind her as it smoothly wove in between the other branches which seemed to grow in length the whole time. In truth, Abby had no idea how big it was to begin with. In her head it was snake size, which at that point in time would probably have been a good thing.

Abby quickly lay flat on the ground as she heard the branch lash out once more. She was half-expecting some hands to burst through the ground and grab her as she avoided the whip. Brilliant, she thought. Getting post-traumatic stress already. The branch missed and Abby continued to journey forward as it was impossible to go back. Not that she would with that thing behind her, but also there was no room to turn without trying some kind of ungainly gymnastic roll that would end with her impaling herself on a branch.

There was still no sign of an opening ahead. However the light in the woods hadn't improved, so Abby may not have been able to see one even if it was there. Fortunately the light hadn't got any worse either, although that didn't really change anything. Either way she was stuck in the middle of the woods, unable to see much, and being chased by a rogue snake-like branch not knowing whether there was an exit or not.

It dawned on Abby that she actually had no clue how big this forest was. For whatever reason she had assumed it was just a line of trees separating one field from another, but she'd been in here far too long for that. What had made her think that it was only a line? Normally that's the sort of thing she'd have considered. But then normally she wasn't being chased by zombies after surviving a skeleton arm attack with wolf howls in the background.

The branch took advantage of Abby's lack of concentration and whipped her side. "Ow!" Abby shouted at the top of her voice feeling the sting of the whip. She wanted to reach back and hold her side hoping it would relieve some of the pain, but she had to keep going forward. She had to get out of this fucking stupid illogical wood. Abby crawled faster reaching a speed which almost felt like running. It turned out she was quite a natural crawler. Who knew?

Abby could feel the warm blood trickling from her side. Again she fought the urge to reach back and grab the wound knowing she couldn't possibly crawl on one arm no matter how good she appeared to be at it. She wondered how serious the injury was. The branch looked razor sharp and had definitely drawn blood, but it didn't feel like it had tried to cut her in half. Was it just toying with her? After all she had nowhere to go. Maybe the sadistic branch knew there was no way out of here and wanted to take its time. Fortunately for Abby that forlorn thought was instantly dismissed.

Light broke the darkness ahead revealing an opening just as Abby caught sight of a second branch tracking her movements. A third quickly joined the chase. Abby was now getting whipped from three different directions, unable to dodge them all as she continued her crawl. It was quickly turning into a public lashing in the private dark dank horrible woods. Fortunately for Abby the lashes felt more like nasty slaps than knife-piecing slashes. Unfortunately for her, it still hurt like hell. She didn't have a moment to enjoy the possibilities of what the light ahead meant, Abby just had to keep crawling as fast as she could.

More moonlight crept through the branches above her as the dead trees began to thin out. Abby was just a few more crawls away from being able to stand. Behind her the moving branches were gathering. Their numbers had increased and now there were about twenty of them sliding through the normal non-moving branches. If they all hit her at the same time she'd know about it at best. At worse, she wouldn't make that opening or any other.

Abby jumped to her feet as the room above her head grew. There were no more branches ahead now, just a clear as day opening, despite it still being night. She sprinted towards it with everything she had left. Blood still trickled from her side as the pain increased with her new upright stretched position. Her back hurt after the multiple lashes and Abby's blood-soaked vest top stuck to it. If she'd taken a proper look at her arms and legs she would have seen every shade of purple possible as well, with a lot of the nastier looking bruises already beginning to turn an even nastier shade of black. All in all she was lucky to be escaping the woods alive, although she wasn't out yet.

Abby took a curious glance back to see how many branches were chasing her in time to see a whole fucking tree literally bounding after her. All the branches belonged to the one tree, and now that one tree seemed aware she was getting away. If the tree had a face it would probably have been smiling seconds earlier as it was having a great time whipping the hell out of her. That joyous occasion was over though, and now it would probably have a more annoyed look as she really was getting away.

"Seriously, what the fuck is going on? This is getting ridiculous now!" Abby shouted aloud as she sprinted towards the opening turning away in disgust from the vicious tree. The tree was closing at a quick rate but Abby was too far ahead. She burst through the tree line victorious in her race against the evil moving tree. Her win however was short lived as she tumbled down an embarkment that marked the end of the forest.

The Swamp

At the bottom of the embankment sat a swamp. Of course there's a fucking swamp in these creepy woods, Abby thought quietly to herself while lying in the dirt checking for cuts, bruises, and broken bones. She definitely had plenty of nasty cuts and bruises, but fortunately no broken bones. It was a miracle nothing was broken though as she really did look a complete state. Not only was she covered in bruises, but her arms and legs were shredded. The centre piece was a sickening gash to her side while her vest top stuck to her stinging red raw back hiding more unpleasantness. She really had survived a barbaric public lashing, only hers was at the hands of a demented evil tree in a sinister forest. Everything had stopped bleeding now at least, but she didn't dare try and unstick her top.

A thin mist covered the swamp and its environs. The surrounding area, from what Abby could see through said mist, mostly contained the same sort of trees she'd just passed through along with a couple of dead looking bushes. Piles of rubble lay here and there but there was no clear sign as to what they used to be or where they came from. They looked more like they were there for effect. That someone had decided the creepy swamp in the middle of the dead woods containing moving trees wasn't spooky enough and a few piles of small stones were needed to complete the look.

Just in front of Abby at the water's edge, thick wooden planks stuck upright from the swamp. A few more boards lay half-submerged beside them as part of what used to be a platform. The wood was rotted and covered in a green seaweed-like substance. Some rusted nails hidden in the moss were bent back into the wood to make them look more like hooks than nails, while others stuck out like a tetanus shot waiting to happen. The mist gently bent round the former platform wary of moving too close to it.

Abby continued to rest in the dirt while she caught her breath. After all, she had just been beaten half to death and nearly eaten by a demonic tree or something to that effect. She couldn't see any movement in the surrounding area of the forest circling the swamp. No branches slithered in front or behind her. No trees ran full pelt towards her. For whatever reason, the tree chasing her had stopped and presumably disappeared back into the forest. Abby didn't know why but was grateful it had.

She hoped it wasn't something along the lines of the evil tree being scared of this area. She more hoped that it just couldn't get down the embankment. Abby hadn't quite realised how much her heart was racing towards the end of the hunt. Everything seemed to happen a little too quick and Abby was left reacting rather than acting. She wasn't quite sure what more she could have done in the situation but was certain she never wanted to be in it again. That tree was fucking scary, even if she'd only caught a quick glimpse of it. With the adrenaline beginning to dissipate she could feel every bruise and cut on her body that little bit more. It really had done a number on her.

There looked to be another possible opening the opposite side of the swamp but it was hard to tell from Abby's distance. Plus she didn't feel in a rush to check it out despite wanting to be out of this place as soon as possible. If it was an opening, it was even smaller than the last one. If it lead to another forest like the one she'd just been through it would be best to not move at all she thought. Just wait here for this nightmare to end.

This was her new theory. That she'd made it back home from the university and was having the nightmare to end all nightmares. How else could you explain skeleton arms, zombies, moving trees, and her in short shorts? She must have been rattled by her encounter with the Splatploitation Brothers and just got indoors and fallen straight asleep with her mind still going crazy over the experience. She fucking hated the whole, 'and it was all just a dream,' endings when she saw them on TV shows, or in movies, but at this precise moment in time it definitely felt like the best outcome. One she could get behind.

Her eyes drifted to the filthy swamp before her. The mist still lightly dusted the top of the disgusting brown water as it continued to steer clear of the broken platform. More of the green seaweed like substance floated on top of the brown water giving the swamp a very earthy colour to it. If the swamp had been in the middle of the woods within the trees you could have easily stepped into it thinking it was the ground. But being at the bottom of the embankment and away from the forest marked it out as something different, which Abby was grateful for. The last thing she could have handled back in that dense claustrophobic forest was falling into some deep foul-looking swamp.

The swamp smelt like a mixture of cut grass and farm. Abby wasn't sure if that's what a swamp should smell like though having never actually seen one in person. She had no real reason to question the smell, but everything about this particular swamp felt a little off in Abby's opinion. Despite not exactly being an authority on the subject. The texture of the green moss didn't look like what she'd expect to find in a swamp either. Plus there was something strangely unsettling about the mist. Even the broken platform didn't have the right feel about it. She couldn't put her finger on it, but something truly wasn't right about this swamp. It felt to Abby like a swamp drawn from memory rather than an actual swamp. But again, what the hell did she know about swamps?

In the middle of the swamp a bubble began to slowly form. It wasn't a normal water bubble either. It appeared thicker, murkier. It may have been caused by the water itself, but Abby was starting to realise that this place didn't work like that. Wherever she was there appeared to be danger all around her, so she wasn't about to take any chances with a bubble, especially when it too felt odd.

The bubble continued to grow at a painstakingly slow rate. Why did everything in this weird graveyard, forest, swamp area take so long? She was grateful it did for the most part but was also growing increasingly impatient about everything. The bubble continued to slowly expand as Abby climbed to her feet realising she'd been on the deck for far too long. Not only that, but she also wanted to be ready to run at a moment's notice if this turned out to be anything more than a bubble, or a small cute frog. Not that she knew where she'd run too. Probably just circle the swamp over and over until she collapsed in exhaustion and got eaten. It wasn't a solid plan.

The bubble quietly popped after growing around a foot in height and the swamp returned to its calm, but somewhat unnatural demeanour. The forest surrounding the swamp was also eerily quiet. No branches were moving, no trees were sprinting towards her. Abby hadn't seen any zombies or skeletons since leaving the graveyard and whatever was howling had lost its voice. But none of this was a comfort as the swamp really was just far too quiet for everything to be ok. She briefly wondered if there were any birds or small animals, but the thought anything could live in that forest seemed silly. Except human eating trees of course.

Some of the bruising on Abby's arms had already began to fade after looking pretty scary not that long ago. Surely that wasn't how bruises worked? She was also relieved that the pain which came with them had subsided too. She unstuck the vest top from her back without tearing any skin off, which was a bonus. The mini recovery didn't really make sense, but nor did anything else, and at least this mystery had been to her advantage. Even the cut to her side seemed to have shrunk and started to heal while she had rested, although that one did still hurt.

A second bubble slowly formed a few metres ahead of where the first had appeared. It began to gradually expand, albeit quicker than the first, and soon passed the height of the original bubble. The bubble was the same colour as the water, a dirty sewage brown with green specks. As Abby carefully watched the bubble for any nefarious signs, it popped. Like the first the pop was silent, as if the air had been sucked out of the bubble rather than someone putting a pin in it.

Ripples had begun to form in the water too. Just a small ripple to begin with, barely noticeable if it hadn't been in the exact spot of the second bubble and therefore at where Abby was directly looking. Abby watched as a second ripple quickly joined it, and then a third. They moved faintly across the water gradually getting bigger the whole time while not creating any sound. The three ripples followed each other to the banks of the swamp. Abby waited for the possibility of something bursting from swamp, but nothing happened when the ripples touched the edge. A joke without a punchline.

A third bubble formed. This one grew much quicker than the previous two. It was accompanied by more ripples which, like the bubble, formed faster than their predecessors. The bubble grew and grew with seemingly no end in sight. The ripples rapidly hit the edges of the swamp firing out wave after wave as they shot from the massive bubble. The swamp was beginning to turn more action-packed with the slow methodical approach now recklessly abandoned in favour of something more akin to a wave pool. A filthy, disgusting, probably diseased-ridden wave pool, but a wave pool nonetheless.

The bubble continued to grow along with the circumference

of the ripples, and the bubble itself neared the edge of the swamp. If it continued to grow much bigger there wouldn't be any room left for the ripples. Abby took a giant step back. She risked a quick glance behind her at the forest and was thankful there were no evil tree creatures waiting for her.

The ripples turned into bigger waves splashing on the swamp banks in an attempt to make the most of the limited room as the bubble began to pulsate. Abby stood watching the swamp show unaware of what else she should do. The bubble was now close to being the whole length and width of the swimming pool sized swamp so her only real escape route was running back the way she came and well, fuck that.

The waves continued to splash over the edge of the swamp sending the foul disgusting water onto the equally dirty looking mud around the swamp. The bubble meanwhile continued to pulsate but it felt to Abby like it had somewhat retracted. It was as if the bubble had realised it had gone too far and not left any room for the wave effect or itself. It was all still far too quiet for Abby as well considering what was happening, not that she was entirely sure what exactly was happening.

Then it all came to an abrupt stop. The bubble burst and the waves became ripples before the ripples became nothing. The whole swamp had had its plug pulled and gone back to its original state.

"That was all rather anticlimactic," Abby told the swamp with almost a hint of disappointment in her voice.

But then a new bubble formed and began to dart straight towards her…

Swamp Boy

The water stirred all around the new bubble as it darted straight towards Abby. She quickly looked around for a possible weapon but there wasn't much on offer. Her choices consisted of a few thin broken branches or some small loose rocks that looked more like paperweights. The better weapon would have been one of the planks of wood from the platform in front of her but the bubble was going to reach the platform before her. Once again Abby was at a disadvantage.

Before Abby could widen her weapon search the bubble leapt from the swamp, or rather what was under the bubble leapt. The bubble itself just burst in mid-air as the creature beneath pierced it. It looked like the exact opposite of catching a Pokémon. Abby wasn't armed, was still in some pain, and really just wanted to sit back down, but she'd survived too much already to give up now. Abby stood ready but regretted not at least picking up one of the small rocks as she caught a blurred glimpse of what lay within the swamp when it landed in front of her.

It took her eyes a moment to adjust before she could see it in all its hideous glory. What the fuck is that? That was the only thought in Abby's head as she stared at the most confusing of creatures. The creature, or rather monster as it was meant to be, was around six feet tall and looked like a person in an awful rubber suit. It looked ridiculous. Abby was certain she'd seen scarier things in a happy meal.

She didn't want to laugh at it, and knew she was meant to be scared of it, but she just wasn't. It had big saucepan-shaped eyes and a tiny nose and mouth, with big pointy ears protruding from halfway down its face. Unlike most slimy creatures she'd seen in movies or read about in books, this one had hair. The hair was the same greenish brown seaweed colour from the swamp. Same texture as well. Abby had been confused by the moss when she first reached the swamp, now she wondered whether it wasn't moss in the water at all, but shredded hair from this pitiful looking monster. The random patches of baldness throughout the monster certainly suggested it was indeed moulting.

If its face was weird, then its body could only be described as downright bewildering. It seemed at first like the monster had the same sort of scale structure as the *Creature From the Black Lagoon*, only completely fucking wrong. Like someone had put Gill Man's suit on upside down. The scales all stuck awkwardly upwards and the fin protruded from the front of the monster rather than its back. How was it meant to swim with a set-up like that? Did it have to constantly backstroke? Abby was certain if she looked at the back of the creature it would have had some abs or something else meant to be at the front. Had this monster been born the wrong way round, or was it meant to look like this? As she'd never seen anything like it before it was hard to tell, but she heavily suspected this monster was just plain wrong.

While Abby stared at the monster it revealed another part of itself as shell-like claws grew from its knuckles. She imagined the pitch for the creature being something along the lines of Gill-Man meets Wolverine, only really, really shit, and upside down. Oh! and back to front. That brought a brief smile to her face when really she should have been paying attention to the bizarre critter.

The monster lunged forward with its long thin lanky scaled covered legs and took a swing at Abby with its shelled claws. Abby noticed far too late as the right claw scratched her lip and sent blood instantly spilling from it. Her eyes watered from the sting of the swipe. The creature then swung its whole arm in an attempt to club Abby rather than just claw her, but she'd learnt her lesson. She bent under the creatures arm and took another big step back towards the ominous forest behind her even though she had no intention whatsoever of returning too it. Despite the cut lip Abby felt she'd still much rather try and run past this mess of a creature than risk coming face to face with that moving evil demented psychotic tree again. She was certain it was just lurking at the top of the embankment awaiting her retreat even if she couldn't see it.

Abby felt the blood on her lips as she patted at the injury. She wiped the blood away along with the tears that had begun to form in the corners of her eyes. Part of her wanted to cry. She couldn't recall ever being hit to the point of bleeding before, yet she'd now faced it twice in the same night. What the fuck was this place and why was it so intent on hurting her? If it was a nightmare or a drug induced dream, why was she causing herself pain? If it was something else, then why did everything want to fuck her up? She sucked back any forthcoming tears determined not to let the ridiculous creature, or this awful place, beat her.

The monster took another lazy swing and Abby once again ducked it. He snarled at her with his thin tiny mouth as Abby saw his teeth for the first time. They were jagged like a set of piranha teeth and most definitely the scariest part of this B-movie monster. As if the monster could feel Abby finally being scared of a part of him he jerked his head forward trying to take a bite out of her arms as she left them hanging defensively in front of her. He made sure to show her all his sharp pointy teeth for a prolonged period of time as the bite missed. It was practically a pose, and not one Abby was impressed by.

Abby pulled her arms back in time as the pose ended with another snap forward from the creatures mouth. The ridiculous fish creature lame Wolverine monster seemed to enjoy that.

Once again he displayed his full set of serrated teeth with a hint of what could have been a smile.

"What the fuck are you meant to be?" Abby aggressively asked while avoiding a third attempted bite. Much to her surprise the creature answered.

"Swamp Boy," it said in a loud whisper back that was neither intimidating or particularly audible. It sounded like he was talking through a bubble in his throat which judging by his arrival could very well have been the case.

"I'm sorry, what?" Abby replied. She failed completely to hide her mocking tone with the tears now long gone and a confidence growing back inside her despite still keeping an eye on the savage-looking teeth the creature displayed at every opportunity.

Swamp Boy cleared his throat with two half coughs that reminded Abby of a cat coughing up a fur ball before it repeated itself with slightly more conviction.

"Swamp Boy," it hissed, a little more audibly.

"That's fucking stupid," Abby curtly replied as she began to circle round him.

Swamp Boy began walking in a circle too with Abby now closer to the platform and Swamp Boy closer to the forest. He seemed somewhat taken aback by Abby's mocking of his name. She could see in his eyes that she'd hurt his feelings, but then he'd cut her lip, so fair's fair.

"So what are you meant to be?" She asked while gesturing his whole body like he was a joke.

Swamp Boy again picked up on the mocking judgemental tone and didn't much care for it.

"Swamp Boy," he answered failing to create any real power or authority in his voice much to Abby's bemusement.

"Can you say anything else?" she asked while edging a little closer to the eroded platform. Swamp Boy had stopped showing his teeth and instead looked at Abby in a manner that suggested he didn't understand why she wasn't scared of him. In truth she was a little, but being mean was one of Abby's primary self-defence mechanisms and Swamp Boy had earned the insults with his assault on her. Plus it seemed to be working. He wasn't used to people not being utterly terrified of him so was at somewhat of a loss as to what to do next.

Abby reached behind for any loose planks of wood stood up in the swamp as she came in line with the platform and took a few more subtle steps back towards it. She kept eye contact with his big saucepan eyes the whole time unsure how dumb or intelligent he was. Abby didn't want to take any chances despite her gut instinct telling her that he definitely wasn't the sharpest knife in the draw. She tried to remain vigilant and careful of his claws too as he still seemed eager to use them despite all the recent mouth posturing.

"I'm going to kill you," it spat out rather unsure of its own statement but feeling like he needed to try and get her scared again. Abby wasn't sure whether the creature didn't believe he could or was uncertain if it wanted too. Either way, much like when the Splatploitation Brothers invaded her editing suite, she wasn't exactly shaking in her boots. That said, that didn't turn out too well for her so she wasn't going to take any chances.

"What have I done to deserve that?" Abby replied in a cutesy manner that didn't suit her at all. If she had a choice to say it in that manner again she definitely wouldn't have. How embarrassing. However it did give her enough time to snatch a decent size piece of wood from the platform. She must have looked very odd grabbing it behind her back from Swamp Boy's perspective but he didn't seem to notice or care, or maybe was just too dumb to realise what she was doing.

"You must die," he said in a robotic-type whisper still sounding very unsure of himself. Was he battling his conscience? Or still uncertain whether he was capable of it? His teeth definitely were, and his claws had already caused some damage, but Abby was starting to get the impression that maybe he didn't want to harm her anymore. That said, his words were saying he did so she kept a very close eye on his every movement while forming a plan of her own.

"I am Swamp Boy," he repeated once again like he had run out of things to say but wanted to carry on the conversation.

Abby continued her circling as she headed back towards the forest side of the swamp. Swamp Boy showed her his claws and teeth once more like he was playing with her. Suddenly he seemed to have a little extra confidence about him, like he had decided after all he could kill her. That he was in control, and she was just some 'frightened little girl.' He practically told so in another one of his loud whispers. She wasn't sure why he had thought that, what had suddenly changed his mind, but his growth in confidences was nothing compared to Abby's. If he really did believe she was some petrified little girl waiting to die, he was wrong.

The second Swamp Boy had his back to the water once more Abby jumped forward and cracked him hard with the plank of wood in her hands. Two rusty nails which stuck from the plank of wood connected with the side of Swamp Boy's head as well as the force of the wood itself. The first nail was one of the bent, hook like nails, and left a nasty imprint on his pointy ear. The nail slightly higher up however wasn't bent out of shape in the least and pierced Swamp Boy's skull with alarming ease.

Abby let go of the plank with it still stuck to the side of Swamp Boy's head. She hadn't realised there were nails in the wood, let alone ones that were strong and long enough to stick into his head and stay there. For a moment she wanted to help the feeble creature, but then remembered he had threatened to kill her on more than one occasion within their brief time of knowing each other. That included just moments before she swung the two by four.

Swamp Boy stood somewhat dumbfounded by the attack. He either hadn't registered exactly what had happened, or she'd broke him. The wooden plank stuck from his skull in an almost comical manner, like it was straight from some sketch with his lack of a reaction completely selling the joke. But this was no comedy sketch, and Swamp Boy certainly wasn't trying to sell anything. He began to wobble as he stared blankly at Abby and struggled to keep his balance as he teetered on the edge of the swamp.

Abby wasn't aggressive by nature, but she was someone who believed in protecting herself. She saw an opportunity to maybe end this fight and took it. Stepping forward she booted Swamp Boy in the chest sending him splashing back into the disgusting swamp. He hit a few more planks of discarded wood from the platform on the way back down which finally loosened the original plank embedded in his skull, not that it made any difference at this point.

With that he sunk under the dirty water and out of sight. Abby peered over the bank of the swamp careful not to get too close, but also curious as to whether it was the end of the battle. She saw no signs of him re-emerging. No bubbles, ripples, or claws grabbing at the broken platform. Or worse, her ankle. Nothing. She wanted to smile, she'd survived. But in truth she was a little disappointed in herself as it dawned on her that she'd probably just killed for the first time in her life. Not including the skeleton and zombies she massacred earlier of course.

A Moments Rest

Everything felt still. The swamp, the forest, Abby. For the first time since she arrived at this wretched place she didn't feel in any immediate danger. It wouldn't last of course, but she was somewhat grateful for the respite. Only somewhat grateful mind you as she shouldn't have been in this unknown dangerous nasty evil land in the first place, and only a few seconds earlier some hideous creature of the deep had been trying to kill her.

"Ok you've had your fun," Abby shouted to anyone who was listening.

"Been good effects too," she pointed at the swamp, "up until this one." Luckily Swamp Boy hadn't resurfaced so didn't hear her mocking tone once more.

There was still no reply. Abby wasn't sure if she expected one or not.

"If you guys are shooting some movie without me knowing then someone needs to come and help the stuntman." She looked down towards the swamp. Still no sign of Swamp Boy. If he was a guy in an upside down rubber suit as Abby theorised then he'd have surely drowned by now. Wasn't so much as a bubble coming from the eerily still swamp which not too long ago acted like a fucking bubble machine.

She didn't exactly care for his well-being, Abby was more just anxious about the whole situation. She had definitely recognised something in him towards the end that had suggested he didn't want to hurt her anymore. She thought she caught a glimpse of sorrow or something as she Spartan kicked him into the swamp. An almost human look backed up her guy in the suit theory. But if that was the case, why wasn't anyone helping him?

Abby waited for an answer, for some movement, for Percy to

yell cut and for the stuntman to burst from the water struggling for breath with his brain still intact. She got none of that, just silence. Abby began to slowly circle the lake. If she was in her apartment she'd be pacing, but she had more room here. She wasn't quite sure what to do with herself, but knew she just needed to be moving. All her best ideas came when she was on the move and at the moment she could do with some kind of inspiration. Nothing was forthcoming.

"You know you're all in serious trouble, right?" Abby gazed down at her skimpy clothes letting them take over as her source of anger once more so she didn't need to face the consequences of whatever just happened with that thing.

"Serious fucking trouble," she mumbled, consigned to not getting an answer.

Abby looked up at the sky. The moon was still low and impossibly bright. It was a sight she'd rarely seen before. Maybe once or twice in her life had she caught a super moon but she'd never really paid attention to it. Or the sky had been filled with clouds so she hadn't bothered trying. This moon was crystal clear. Despite the brightness she felt she could see every detail within it, or maybe her mind was filling in the blanks. Every crater and dent seemed to be fully formed. Like the highlights had all been restored. It really was a remarkable sight, if not somewhat unrealistic.

The night air was still warm. Despite the skimpy clothes she hadn't felt cold since she arrived here, and Abby often felt cold. Warmth wise there was no need for her hoodies, comfort wise on the other hand was a different issue. She'd lost all track of time long ago to the point where she couldn't even hazard a guess, but it didn't feel as though the moon was in any rush to go and the sun still hid away. She suppressed a yawn before wondering whether that yawn was real or not, like she was in the *Matrix* or something and deciding on the taste of chicken.

Her mind once again began to try and piece things together.

"So how'd you do it? You sickos drug my coffee?" Again there was no response from the night. The forest remained still and quiet with no signs of anyone. If the Splatploitation Brothers were lurking in the woods they'd stopped all the ridiculous banging of doors and stamping around noises and suddenly become fucking ninjas.

"Just give me some kind of answer here. I don't understand any of this," Abby called out with her voice breaking and tears threatening to emerge. She tried to calm herself, again determined not to show any weakness. She didn't want them to have the satisfaction, but she really was starting to feel desperate for any kind of hint or answer.

"So is it a dream?" She casually asked.

"A hallucination?" She added before even waiting for an answer from the first question.

"Where am I really at the moment? Because if this isn't some kind of set and I'm dreaming this, where have you stashed me?" She wasn't sure if she wanted to know the answer to that one. Abby didn't much like the idea of being unconscious around those guys, no one would. She was just thinking aloud at this point. Although if she was dreaming why would they be in her dream to answer a question she didn't know the answer too. Her brain was starting to feel fried.

But she was sure she wasn't dreaming. Well not sure, but something told her she wasn't. Everything felt too real in a sense. Not real real, because of the zombies and swamp monsters, but she could feel the pain from the lashes and the blood from her cut lip. Even the warm night time air felt authentic, if somewhat unfeasible in Abby's eyes. Every sensation she felt was different from any dream or nightmare she had ever had before. In those she could feel the emotion of the situation, and maybe a reaction, but not the actual sensation of it all. She'd never felt the wind in a dream, or warmth, or the taste of blood in her mouth.

So if this wasn't a set, which was unlikely because it was way too fucking good for the Splatploitation Brothers to start with, and also that stuntman would be dead by now, then what was it? Not a dream or nightmare. Could drugs do this? Abby had tried a little weed before and had eaten a hash-brownie once that made her paranoid as fuck, but she'd never felt close to any kind of hallucination of this level. Is this what other drugs could do? The ones she had no inclination to try.

She knew that mushrooms and LSD could make you hallucinate, but surely not to this level of realism. She'd have heard about it if it was like this. How long did that shit last anyway? she thought. She'd been here a while now. Also why did she have this blank space in her mind from when she landed in the pit? And why the fuck was she wearing different clothes? None of it made sense.

Abby had been trying to piece together what had happened from the pit onwards and felt no closer to the truth. For all she knew she'd guessed right a few times as the same ideas were repeating in her head, but no one seemed to be around to tell her whether she was right or wrong. Did she just have to let this all play out and hope at some point she'd wake up in her bed and admonish herself for having such a weird fucked-up nightmare? But what if this wasn't some hideous nightmare or drug-induced dream, would she just let it play out forever?

Abby hated not being in control. She was a writer, a director, and a loner. Everything she did was in her control. If she succeeded it was because of her; if she failed or procrastinated it was because of her. Almost all of her daily actions were based around her being in control. She had none of that here. Did she even have free will? Because no fucking way would she normally have gone through that forest, not without considering it a lot more, slow-moving zombies behind her or not.

Was she thinking about this all too much? She'd been accused of that plenty in her life. By her very nature, she was an over-thinker. But if you were ever going to overthink something, surely this was the type of situation that you would. She just wanted some kind of answer, some direction, some clue as to what was happening and how long it would continue. Hell she'd settle for knowing if this was still the same day or what the time was at this point.

"Wake the fuck up Abby," she screamed, even subjecting herself to a sharp slap across the face like they do in the movies to wake someone from a trance.

She wanted to laugh at herself when she considered that she'd already been hit, choked, and lashed plenty tonight. If slapping was going to work it would have done so already.

'Why you hitting yourself?" She mumbled in a juvenile voice bringing a rare smile as she tried to break the tension she was putting on herself. At least that's how she reasoned it. She may have just been cracking the fuck up.

Abby had paced the length of the swamp without realising. Just in front of her lay a pathway out of the woods. It was as clear as day, a dirt path leading out of the swamp without having to go through the whatever they are trees again. Abby was sure she'd scoped out this whole area when she was laying at the bottom of the embankment, positive she had in fact, and at no point had there been an easy access path out of this place. That's the sort of thing she would most definitely have noticed.

"This wasn't here before," she said talking to herself while pointing at the exit. She'd remembered noticing a possible opening before, but it didn't look like this. At best it was a teeny gap in between the trees which she had no fucking intention whatsoever of going through. This looked ready-made for a nice woodland stroll. She gawked at it for a few moments more, confusion mixed with mistrust. She shook her head at the clearing wholeheartedly disbelieving in its very existence. It had trap written all over it.

"What happens when I step on the path?" Abby asked extremely sceptically. "More zombies? Skeleton arms burst from the ground? Shitty looking dinosaurs?"

As had become customary this evening there was no answer. Abby dipped a toe onto the pathway as though testing the temperature of the water at the beach. Nothing happened. She slowly crept her whole foot on to the dirt path. Still safe. She pulled it back while suspiciously eyeing the trees either side of the walkway. None of them appeared to be moving. They all still looked as evil as sin and like they wanted to kill her given the chance, but they all remained rooted to their spot. Her foot crept on to the path once more still without consequence.

Abby put her foot on and off the path like a child being told to not touch something but touched it anyway. She had a childish side to her that she hid from everyone but this probably wasn't the time to show that. She couldn't help herself though. To most Abby was a pretty serious person, and she was, but she enjoyed these little fun moments she shared only with herself. Like dancing when no one is looking or telling a bad joke to yourself and laughing. It was a warm side of her which never ever went public and now really wasn't the time to indulge it, despite it being kind of sweet.

"Fuck it," Abby finally said and stepped on to the dirt path that lead her through the forest but away from the evil-looking trees. For once nothing jumped out at her or stalked her. It really was just a very, very convenient path leading away from the swamp and everything else she'd passed through. A little too convenient.

Unknown Land

Abby's stroll through the forest via the newly formed path led her to an old wooden fence at the bottom of a slight hill. She had been nervous the whole walk, just waiting for something to spring out, or swoop down on her, but nothing did. The lack of being attacked had definitely made her more cautious and paranoid of the fence she'd come across. More than a fence normally would. This was mostly because she'd never felt threatened by a fence before, but more relevant to her current situation, it was because she knew the next thing trying to fucking eat her had to be right around the corner. That's just the way the night had been going.

The wooden fence looked battered by the elements. The wood was rotten and discoloured, the posts crumbling. The barbed wire wrapped around the fence was rusted and hung loose. The grass on the outside of the fence was overgrown and there were loose branches and twigs scattered everywhere. The loose branches belonged to the foreboding forest Abby had just walked through, but despite still looking sharp and evil, they lacked a lot of their threat while lying helplessly on the ground. That said, she wouldn't have been shocked at this point if one of them started to slither towards her.

Further along the fence to Abby's right, there was an equally neglected metal gate. Much like the barbed wire the gate was rusted, but to a more extreme proportion. Only a few silver specks remained. Everything else on the gate was a nasty-looking brown colour with blotches all over it. There had been nothing fancy about the gate, even in its prime, and was just a normal long swing gate leading to the land beyond, but now it looked like it had always been this eyesore. Born disfigured.

To both sides of the fence, gate, and land beyond, there was nothing but woods. More dark vicious looking trees with their extra pointy branches. These trees at least seemed to have some leaves but they were all dark and dead looking too. Nothing about these woods said come through me. Not that the land beyond the gate and fence was remotely inviting, but compared to the woods, and what Abby knew lurked inside them, the land ahead seemed a better option. Abby had increasingly found herself making choices this way, the lesser of two evils had become her North Star.

It wasn't even a coin toss, or a rock, paper, scissors situation, just that way looks less fucking scary and demented than this way. Abby hated having to make decisions in this manner. It felt like they were out of her control, despite her being the one to make them. As if she was being manipulated. Like the ideas were being planted in her head but made to feel like her own. That's not how Abby operated and she'd grown increasingly frustrated at this wicked game she didn't want to play. She wondered for a moment why she used the word 'game,' but the thought slipped from her mind before she really addressed it.

Closer to the gate Abby spotted a sign lying on the floor. It was face down next to the hole in which it once stood. Abby reached down and turned the sign over careful not to snag herself on the barbed wire wrapped around it. The sign read, 'Keep Out. Private Property.' A bit cliché Abby thought. Not sure what she expected it to say, but she should heed its warning. Abby let the sign drop back to the ground still being wary of the barbed wire.

She tried opening the rusty gate while being careful not to get any metal splinters or anything that may have required some kind of shot. The gate didn't open easily however as it caught on the jagged ground beneath a few times. Eventually, Abby managed to yank it open after coming close to giving up and climbing over the top instead, something she really didn't fancy doing with her bare legs on display and the gate looking almost disease-ridden. Entering the unknown land instantly felt like a stupid idea, but what other options did she have? Much like the graveyard it really did feel like there was just one option. Private property and ominous entry or not, she had to go forward.

Abby had never really been one for misguided adventures. She liked hill climbing and trekking, and would gladly travel the world if possible, but sneaking on to private property or into unknown areas wasn't her thing. She was curious by nature, but not a thrill seeker. She enjoyed the type of adventure where you knew what the adventure was beforehand, but the mystery element never appealed to her. She'd already faced several unknown dangers this evening and wasn't looking forward to the next, yet knew another one was likely ahead. Still, any second thoughts of turning back were dispelled when she looked back to the creepy forest. No fucking way was she going back in there.

The grass inside the land was dead. Dried up to the point where there was no colour or life left in any of the blades. Random pieces of corroded wood lay amongst the dead grass with no indication of what they might once have belonged to. The land was built on a slope that was slowly revealing more and more of itself as Abby ascended. She looked back to see the woods disappearing from sight. It hadn't felt like she'd walked far enough for it to already be a dot in the distance, but she supposed the slope helped with that. The geography of the land already felt disconcerting, nevertheless, the woods disappearing did bring a sigh of relief.

A few paces in front of Abby a broken metal bucket rested on the ground. One half of the bucket was torn away only leaving a small serrated edge towards the bottom. Inside the bucket sat some dark bloody mouldy fur, possibly belonging to a large rat or something similar. Abby didn't get close enough to find out.

As she walked past the bucket she noticed a bloody hand-print across the other side. She instantly became more alert and cautious. She could feel her shoulders tensing, her stomach tightening. This quiet period was beginning to get to her.

Everything she'd seen so far in this nightmarish land had at least all been monsters and ghouls. This handprint clearly looked human. It was impossible to tell if it belonged to a victim, a killer, or was just some kind of accidental cut due to the jagged metal, but every bit of it screamed evil intentions. Abby wished she had a bat or something to protect herself with, even if she couldn't put a face to the danger yet.

The next reveal from the hill's slope was a decaying shelter that stood alone with nothing around it. It looked like it started life as a bus shelter, yet here it stood, just barely upright in some unknown land. The plastic panels from the shelter were long gone, while the roof was hanging down from the metal framework. If there had been any sides they weren't there anymore. Piled up within the exposed shelter was a stack of animal carcasses. They looked to be in the latter stages of decay from what Abby could tell. They may have been cows but were too far gone to be sure.

The ground beneath the dead animals was scorched despite the animals themselves not looking like they had ever been burnt. Maybe this was a regular dumping ground? More roadkill lay in the brown grass surrounding the shelter. The smell caught Abby with a full blast as a gush of wind hurried by. Abby lifted her top a little to cover her nose but instantly hated how much skin that led to being shown. She chose to put up with the smell rather than risk running into someone with her midriff on display. There hadn't been a wind at any point up until now. Appalling timing, Abby thought.

Something crunched on the ground beneath Abby causing her to look down and see a pile of bones. She couldn't tell if they were human or animal, but they didn't attack her so that was a bonus. Unlike the animal carcasses, these bones had been scraped clean of any and all skin and remains. Nothing but bones here. Abby wasn't certain if that was reassuring or not. She kept a watchful eye on them as she passed by expecting them to crawl after her at any given moment. Luckily they just remained as a static pile of bones in the middle of an unnerving field.

The dead grass finally started to show some signs of change a little further ahead of Abby, only it wasn't grass. Rows and rows of dry corn stalks stuck from the ground. They were a similar colour to the grass and stood a few feet taller. The moonlight showed no life in any of the corn as they all appeared withered and brown. The cobs were flaky and hung open and exposed. No one had tended this field for a long time. The unknown land was still feeling very abandoned, but Abby knew better than to think that was the case. The piled-up corpses and rows of corn meant something had once been here and knowing Abby's luck, it still lurked somewhere nearby.

Abby started to walk through the cornfield greatly aware that all the horror convention knowledge she possessed meant that no fucking way whatsoever should she ever be walking through a cornfield, let alone in the dead of night under a full moon. The review she would have given this film, and the dumb lead girl strolling through it, would have been scathing. But living it, she wasn't sure what else she could do. Whatever waited for her at the end of this cornfield, or just beyond it, or within it, she was meant to meet. She couldn't have gone any other way at any other point that wouldn't have led to some other nasty situation and probable death. No, she knew walking through a cornfield, on an abandoned farm at the dead of night under this ridiculous bright full moon was inviting death, but she really truly believed it was her only choice. Which made her question again whether it even counted as a choice.

As she stepped over more bones that fortunately didn't attack her Abby noticed a scarecrow standing in the middle of the cornfield. The clothes on the scarecrow felt Jack the Ripper inspired. He had a tall tatty black hat that was half falling off and half somewhat remarkably staying on his head, along with a long black cloak. The cloak was riddled with holes that the moonlight leaked through making the scarecrow look even more terrifying, which was his job after all.

Abby wasn't frightened of scarecrows in the same way that she hated snakes, but she wasn't a fan either. They were like clowns or porcelain dolls to her. Just one of those things where she didn't understand why anyone could like them. They always made her feel uneasy. She took a few steps away from the scarecrow giving it a much wider berth.

She kept her eyes on him as she passed. As much as Abby didn't want to look at the chilling scarecrow she also didn't trust it wouldn't jump out at her. She ended up even more panicked about it when it was out of sight. What if it stuck up behind her? She knew things were due to go south soon and the scarecrow fitted the bill. But he didn't come for her this time.

The main reason for that was because the really real threat lay just ahead. As Abby cleared the last of the dead corn a farmhouse came into view just in front of her. A sign near the front of the house revealed the farm's name, but she already knew it. Abby stood on the edge of Hillbilly Farm.

Rerun

The house was a perfect recreation of Hillbilly Farm. It looked exactly like the house from the film right down to every single detail. Nothing was out of place. The way the roof was sliding off, the broken and boarded windows, the rusty nail-covered planks of wood all over the farmhouse. The tatty door falling off its hinges. All was perfect, so to speak. No doubt about it, this had to be the exact location where the film was shot.

Abby stood for a moment taking it all in. She'd been through a lot that night and didn't think anything else would shock her, but this had. Not that long ago she'd been watching the trashy film and hating every frame of it, and now here she was outside the very house in which the blood-soaked cringe fest took place.

"Too fucking weird," Abby muttered to herself holding back the temptation to rub her eyes in a disbelieving manner as they did in the cartoons.

From her vantage point, Abby could see more of the grounds surrounding the house which hadn't been used in the film. Near to where she stood there was a shooting range with a couple of bullet-riddled silhouetted targets standing at the far end. The holes in the target were all big, maybe fist sized, as if someone had shot the target with a cannon rather than a rifle. The targets themselves weren't the normal silhouetted crooks with guns you always saw either - these targets were teenage girls all looking somewhat provocative and scantily clad even in silhouetted form.

Beyond the house she could see the beginnings of what looked like a boneyard of sorts. She couldn't make out very much except an old truck and a large barn. She didn't care much for the sinister-looking barn, but the truck definitely seemed a good option even though Abby couldn't drive. The still brightly moon-lit sky seemed to be aiming down extra hard on both the truck and the barn highlighting them out against whatever else rested in the boneyard. A detail that wasn't lost on Abby.

Closer to the house Abby could see the outline of the pigpen Whitney died in. It wasn't as well-lit as the truck for whatever reason, it just seemed to wait there hidden in the shadows. If there were pigs inside the sty, they were being very quiet. She squinted her eyes for a better look and felt she saw some movement in the pen but couldn't be sure. Everything had felt too quiet and still for too long now but Abby knew that was all about to change because what was perfectly lit was the farmhouse. Abby's full attention turned to the ominous building.

Abby carefully walked towards a half-boarded window at the side of the house. She tried her best to stay in the few shadows on offer and kept low to the ground hunching over in her walk but was cursing the moon for acting like a giant security light the whole way. Everything in the film showed this farmhouse to be a house of absolute evil and depravity so she wasn't taking any chances.

The sensible thing to do would have been to turn and run the moment she saw the fucking house, but she couldn't will herself to go just yet. She had to peep inside. Despite the film being a piece of shit, she felt a lure to the house, like she had to see it all for herself. It wasn't every day she had the chance to be on location of a film she'd watched, so cringe-worthy or not, Abby felt a need to check everything out. Peek behind the curtain and see the magic so to speak, except she suspected there wouldn't be anything magical about this house.

A bunch of cracked plant pots led to the scratched window. Light from inside the house escaped the part of the window which hadn't been boarded but Abby was still a little too far away to tell if anyone was home. Even the light in the home seemed dirty to Abby, like it seeped through some kind of putrid filter. It was closer to the colour of the dead grass than normal household lighting. Another sure sign to stay the fuck away from the place, but Abby ignored her gut feeling for once. She knew it was wrong to continue, but simply couldn't stop herself. She had to see. Abby wasn't sure if it was her own immense curiosity or whether she'd somehow lost her free will, but either way, she had to glance through the window and see what horrors awaited inside.

Abby was extra careful not to step on any of the pots as she stealthily approached the window. She stopped a few feet away from the house when she finally heard movement inside. Someone was definitely home. Abby knew someone had to be in the house the moment she saw it. Despite everything about the place looking dead and abandoned, it had a kind of sinister vibe to it that felt present rather than past. Abby continued to take every step softly until she reached the half-boarded window. She peered through the worn glass into the farmhouse kitchen intrigued as to what, or who, waited inside.

Who waited inside was none other than Psycho Hillbilly's Mom, the matriarch of Hillbilly Farm. She wore a blood-soaked apron which could have literally been any colour to begin with but was now a deep disgusting filthy red. Her thick greasy grey hair had matted together - small animals could literally live in there. It wasn't much of a guess to say she'd probably never washed her hair in her life and if it had been cut she probably did it herself with a hacksaw without giving a fuck about the outcome.

Her face was scarred all over. Long since healed scars rested on her cheeks and forehead. A larger scar appeared to come from her right eye and join up with one of those by her cheek. Speaking of her eyes, they were a piercing brown colour, narrow and sinister. They'd seen a lot of evil in their life and most of it had come from their owner. Her left eye looked slightly hazy, misted over like the eye could be blind.

Her mouth was thin with her lips pushed tightly together. A sinister curl to her lips dominated the left side of her mouth, the right side looked almost lazy in comparison. Every inch of this woman's face was angry. She was ready to kill at a moment's notice and for any reason she saw fit. She did not look like someone you wanted to fuck with even if she appeared to be a hundred years old and partially blind.

While she might not quite be a hundred she was old, really old, but that didn't seem to hinder her. She was busy preparing something in the kitchen as Abby watched her viciously bring a cleaver down on whatever was resting on the kitchen counter. The cleaver itself was as blood-soaked as the apron the older woman wore and seemed like an extension of her arm by the way she wielded it. The cuts were short and sharp, with precision. She definitely knew how to handle it.

As Hillbilly Mom stepped away from the kitchen counter towards a spice rack on the other side of the room Abby got a better view of what was being chopped… a human leg. Or rather what remained of a human leg. Quite a few cuts had already been taken from the leg as it lay deflated on the kitchen counter. The bone it used to be wrapped around sat a few metres away from the mutated flesh. A cookbook was open next to it but Abby was certain there couldn't possibly be a recipe inside that required a human leg.

If she'd been able to glance inside the book she would have seen that she was wrong. This wasn't any old cookbook, this was Hillbilly Mom's very own cookbook, and a shocking number of recipes inside required some kind of human flesh. You could go as far as to say it was the theme of the book. From the outside, it just looked like any other cookbook with a picture of a pie on the front, although it was hard to tell what was inside the pie. From the rest of the book, you'd be odds on at guessing something human.

A loud bang rocked the house from above the kitchen knocking Abby out of her trance as she continued to stare at the horrors in front of her. The bang was quickly followed by the echoes of wooden steps as someone descended the stairs at full speed. Abby couldn't see who from her vantage point, more just caught a glimpse of the blurred figure as it sprinted past the kitchen door.

"Get that skanky whore," the ghastly woman in the kitchen shouted in a horrific southern accent as the escapee screamed for her life.

Abby slowly repeated the words to herself. She knew that line and that dreadful accent. She had heard it just days before while watching *Hillbilly Farm*. But she hadn't seen this side of it. She hadn't seen the awful woman who shouted, she had been out sight, or rather just out of frame. Abby was now privy to a different angle, a new perspective of the film. Like that brief moment in time when you could choose the camera angles of certain films on DVD, except Abby wasn't standing there with a remote and TV in front of her watching the movie, she was seeing it in person.

"Live action theatre?" She unconvincingly remarked to herself almost dismissing the notion before she had even fully said it.

How could it be that? Too many questions were already sprinting through Abby's head. How on earth would they have done half of these effects to begin with? The skeleton arm alone was impossible. And Swamp Boy? Sure, he looked like a guy in a suit, but he wasn't, was he? If so surely he drowned, or are there more tricks at play? Even the scene in front of her looked real. The leg, the blood-soaked workbench and the apron, it looked real. Worse still it felt real. Although the kitchen wasn't in the finished film Abby could clearly picture what it would have looked like if it were, and it wouldn't have been this. Not this real. Not this lived in. The Splatploitation Brothers were notorious for their poor interior sets and that wasn't even Abby being mean, it was a fact.

This is all ridiculous, she thought. The Splatploitation Brothers are shit, they couldn't possibly pull this off. She couldn't pull this off, and she was a lot smarter than them. But what just happened was straight from the film she had trashed. There was no mistaking what she had just witnessed was a scene from *Hillbilly Farm*, albeit one from a different angle.

Abby shook her head more uncertain than ever. There had been no answers all evening, only more questions, and a lot more confusion. Every theory she came up with just didn't fit, didn't seem plausible, but whatever was happening surely couldn't be possible no matter what the answer. She thought again about how it had to be a dream or a drugged-filled trip. Maybe her subconscious was redirecting the movie, making it better. But why? And how?

She managed to duck in time as Hillbilly Mom returned to the kitchen counter to finish preparing the leg losing interest in whatever had just happened outside the room. Abby watched as the ghastly woman sprinkled some spices over the leg and added some salt and pepper like that's exactly what you're meant to do when preparing to cook a fucking human leg.

Abby could tell the oven was already on. She could see the flame burning brightly inside. It wasn't like any oven Abby had used, not that she'd used many, this one looked like it was on fire, ready to be fed whatever meat came its way. She couldn't see how it would properly cook anything, it seemed more like a furnace ready to incinerate anything shoved in. Hillbilly Mom took the leg from the side and headed towards the flaming oven.

Abby watched as she opened the door unperturbed by the raging flames inside. For her this was just a normal day doing normal things. For Abby it was anything but.

Before she could watch the old hag any further she heard screams emanating from the front garden of the house. She had heard these screams before too. There was no doubt about it, they were coming from Whitney, and if memory served Abby correctly, she was probably on the floor looking down at the mess that used to be her friends right about now.

Pigs and Body Parts

Abby crept around the corner of the house making sure she kept low and out of sight of the kitchen window. She felt like she'd spent the last ten minutes practically crawling on the ground but had no intention of letting anyone on this creepy farm see her until she knew what the fuck was going on. When she finally did poke her head around the corner a few seconds later Abby saw exactly what she expected to see, although that didn't make it any easier to either witness or take in.

Lying on the floor at the end of the garden just like she was in the movie was Whitney. The poor girl looked terrified, but at least she was in a better state than what lay beneath her. Blood and body parts belonging to Whitney's friends covered the end of the garden path just as they had before. A multitude of reds and lumps of flesh all piled together. It looked a lot more real up close than it had in the film. The effects department had really upped their game since the release Abby briefly thought before another unnerving idea entered her mind... Was this somehow real?

It all looked a lot more real now. Everything from the blood on the floor, to the body parts, to the house itself. Even Whitney's acting seemed a lot more genuine in the here and now. In the film she had looked terrified, but in that bad teen horror acting way. Here it seemed more authentic, like she actually was really, really scared and battling to survive. Was her life on the line more than just in the make believe of the movie way?

Abby wanted to dismiss the thought instantly, tell herself she was being stupid, that it wasn't possible, but her insides told her different. Which, if true, meant this girl really was in a lot of trouble and that was actually her friends smeared across the floor. Had Abby stumbled across a snuff movie? This didn't explain how it looked fake in the film she'd already watched though. Was the movie some kind of rehearsal for the real thing? Was this the version that you wouldn't find on Netflix, the one you'd have to search the dark web for instead. Nah, it couldn't be that, could it?

Had Whitney screamed at this point? That scream Abby heard, she knew it was Whitney's, but was that the right moment for her to scream? Or like the kitchen and Hillbilly Mom, was Abby seeing extra? A different take or perspective to what she watched on her TV. Abby wasn't sure if it mattered, but for some reason it did. If this was different from the movie, even slightly, what exactly did that mean? Was her crazy theory about this being the snuff version correct? How did she even get to that conclusion? Abby began to think she was completely losing her mind. It was the best explanation as things stood.

She watched as a pig slowly trotted towards Whitney, and sure enough it had a hand in its mouth. But again it looked and felt different. The hand in the film was obviously a rubber one that you could spot straight away. But this hand, this looked real. It was chewed up the same, and missing the same fingers, but the texture was completely different. More flesh and bone than rubber and latex. Again if it was an effect it was way beyond the normal capabilities of the Splatploitation Brothers. Sure, Roger wasn't the worse effect artist around no matter how much Abby unfairly slated him in her blog, but he wasn't close to being this good either, never would be.

Other pigs followed all with bona-fide looking body parts in their mouths. Something inside Abby began to stir. She started to feel sick. She could watch anything in a movie, rarely ever turned her head, but this was different. Not only did it look more real, but it also felt it too. This was beyond even *Cannibal Holocaust* levels of feeling real. Her hair was standing on end, her mouth was suddenly dry, her stomach tightening. Again she found herself asking the same old question - what the fuck was going on? But the more pressing question had become just how real was this place? Had her imagination added an extra layer of rendering to all the visual effects around her in this nightmare or was this somehow supposedly made-up place starting to feel legit.

None of it made sense and Abby was growing more and more frustrated trying to work it out. She wasn't even sure what she was trying to get at anymore. She didn't know what conclusion she even wanted now as all the answers seemed pretty fucking horrendous. It's all just a dream was still her favourite solution, her best-case scenario, but whatever was going on, it wasn't a dream. Abby knew that much.

Abby's thoughts were interrupted as Psycho Hillbilly emerged from the house. He wore the same outfit as in the film right down to the oil stains and ugly boils. These ones didn't look painted on though, they were part of him. She took a good look at his face and felt surprised to see that it was the same as in the movie, it was Matthew.

The same Matthew that she had kicked in the nuts and dropped to the floor earlier in the evening. Except here, despite his skinny frame and gummy-looking mouth, he had power. She could see it. He wasn't someone to fuck with. He had a menacing grin on his face and held his pitchfork with nasty intent. He stood stronger than Matthew and looked more defined in a way. Matthew was nothing but a whiny little brat, but this guy she'd cross the road to avoid. He was intimidating, where Matthew was about as menacing as Peppa Pig.

But again she had that nagging feeling of how this could be possible. Having met Matthew earlier in the evening she knew this wasn't him. Not a chance. No one can change that much. That pathetic creeper she floored at the university couldn't be this person, not even if he upped his acting a hundredfold. Unlike Roger who did at least have some talent, she knew Matthew couldn't pull off this person standing before her. Sure, he could be the version she saw in the film, easily, because that guy was a plank of wood dressed as a slasher. But this guy was something else altogether. Something Matthew most definitely wasn't. This guy was the real deal.

"I'm going to feed you to the pigs little girl. Oink, Oink, Oink," he told Whitney in his terrible accent. Hearing them both up close Abby was sure her first assessment had been right. His accent sounded worse than his mom's. Although worse was a relative term. Psycho Hillbilly began to stamp towards Whitney with a shit eating grin on his face as the pigs circled around her chewing on their new human food. In the film his walk towards her had felt a little goofy, maybe just because of the way she was viewing the film, or maybe because Matthew was a fucking hack. But again here, up close, it felt a lot more sinister.

Abby turned back round the corner. She sat against the wall holding her knees as she wondered what the hell was happening. This was starting to get way too much now. The dream-like quality of the graveyard and woods was starting to die away and being replaced by, for a lack of a better word, reality. But it couldn't be. She'd seen this as a film. The young girl out there battling for her life was an actress as far as Abby knew. Not a very good one, but an actress all the same. She heard more movement from the garden but didn't need to look. She'd seen Whitney clamber to her feet before. Seen her slip on the blood and body parts of her friends before she somehow escaped the garden only for Psycho Hillbilly to follow her and then…

… Abby peaked back around the corner in time to see Psycho Hillbilly holding a pig aloft in his hand. He pulled it back and aimed it in the direction of Whitney. The pig was struggling for its freedom but couldn't escape. It dropped its human hand chew toy to the floor and starting making plenty of noise as it squealed and grunted. Psycho Hillbilly didn't pay any attention. He was too in the moment. Enjoying himself way too much for someone covered in blood while standing in the remains of a bunch of dead teens holding a pig aloft ready to throw it at the sole petrified survivor.

Abby watched in horror as he launched the pig towards Whitney. It would almost be comical if it wasn't so cruel. The pig bounced off the back of Whitney's head sending her once again tumbling to the floor and making the Psycho Hillbilly break out in hysterics. He was laughing like that was the funniest thing he'd ever seen in his life. He couldn't stop himself. Tears of laughter were streaming down his face, he'd lost all control of his senses. It didn't take long for him to drop to the floor and pound the deck with his fists as he continued to laugh his head off. It was like a cartoonish laugh, except in Abby's eyes, and probably everyone else's for that matter, it wasn't funny in the slightest.

"You guys used a real pig? Abby whispered in a disgusted tone as she saw the pig wobble back to its feet and trot off in what she assumed was a foul and embarrassed mood. Whitney lay on the ground for a moment longer before she too tried to get back to her feet and continue her escape. She hadn't a clue what had happened to her and given the chance to guess probably wouldn't have picked knocked out by a flying pig. She just had tunnel vision for getting the fuck out of here. Abby hadn't seen any of this the first time round as it all happened off-screen. She'd just heard the sound effects, not thinking for a second it had actually played out. She thought it was just a visual gag done in bad taste that she'd turned her nose up at, now she really wished it was just that.

Psycho Hillbilly finally composed himself wiping the last

tears of laughter from his eyes and picked up his pitchfork from the floor. He looked all business once again as if he had snapped back into his menacing role aware that he had broken character with his over-the-top laughter. He remained serious for a brief moment, stern, and then that annoying sickening smile of his returned. He restarted his stalking of Whitney once again looking like the horror slasher he was.

As he left the garden and began to gain on Whitney, Abby came out of hiding. She kept low once more as she circled the garden to reach the end of the path where the mess of Whitney's friends lay. Looking straight at Abby was a decapitated head. She remembered from the film it belonged to a girl called Alice but couldn't remember anything more about her. The character was poorly written and Abby was almost rooting for her death due to her constant stupidity. But seeing her head lying on the floor now several metres away from her body Abby was feeling differently. Mostly due to her very uneasy feeling that this was somehow all real.

Abby knelt down beside the decapitated head. She didn't want to, every part of her told her not to, but she had to know. She had to know whether this head was fake or not. This whole ordeal, despite how unbelievably unreal it seemed, was no longer feeling like a dream or a nightmare. Even the idea of it being some kind of drug trip had faded from her mind. She wasn't sure what any of this was, but she trusted her senses, her gut, and at the moment her gut was telling her this was really happening no matter how implausible.

Abby blanked out what was going on near the pig pen. She could hear the horrible drawl of Psycho Hillbilly and the desperate pleas of Whitney, but for the moment she had pushed those sounds aside. Her hand slowly drifted towards the head lying on the floor. Abby knew if she touched it she'd instantly know whether it was real or not, but deep down Abby already knew the answer. She knew the answer the moment Whitney came flying out of that door and she saw the blood and guts on the floor. But still, she had to confirm it.

She traced her finger along the face of the decapitated girl stroking the side of her cheek. Her fingers got bloody as she continued to examine the formerly beautiful face. Abby was stuck in the action. One touch was all she needed, it was real alright. She was stroking the decapitated head of a young actress on the very set of her last performance. Abby didn't know how the girl ended up here like this, or how she herself got here either, but here on the farm they both where.

Abby withdrew her hand and frantically started wiping the blood on to any piece of the ground not smeared with body parts. She stared at the head for a little longer still unable to fully comprehend what was going on but fully aware that somehow this was real. To her side a new scream emanated, this one catching Abby's attention and breaking her trance. Unlike the last time Whitney died now there was someone around to help her. Someone to save the frightened brutalised girl from that fucking maniac and whatever the fuck all this was.

Abby spotted a spade on the floor and instinctively snatched it. She began her own march in Whitney's direction.

Time to save the day.

Abby The Saviour

Whitney sat on her knees looking up at the deranged Psycho Hillbilly in the middle of the filthy pig pen. His smile covered his whole face as she pleaded for her life and promised to do anything in return. The poor girl was done, broken. She'd been through more in a day than most would have to endure in a lifetime, she'd finally run out of fight. She'd tried to run away but had been stopped. Tried to crawl to safety but had been found. Now she had tried to get to her feet and couldn't, all to the delight of her crazed tormentor who was literally licking his lips at the prospect of what to do next.

He pretended to mull over what her 'I'll do anything' could consist of, but he already knew what he wanted. He'd got all the delight he needed out of torturing and stalking the poor girl, now was the time to finish her off. But how best to do it? And what killer line would complete the job? After all he was a slasher so he needed some style about him. He'd been killing helpless girls for a long time now and had run through all the cool lines and awesome kills he had stored up in his unhinged head. He needed something new, something fresh. He wouldn't want to be seen as getting stale. Plus she'd earned the right to a unique death with a nasty quip.

She had brought him great amusement. I mean how many times in your life do you get to chuck a fucking pig at someone's head and watch them comically topple over? He laughed a little more at the nostalgic memory but quickly composed himself, after all this was serious business. How to kill this helpless worthless pathetic bimbo? How to fuck her up more than he did her friends, which was a tough task considering they were currently staining his pavement.

Whitney offered no resistance while he deliberated. She

really was done. This wasn't how she imagined her life ending, but it wasn't like she had a choice. He had toyed with Whitney and her friends all day. From the moment they were abducted he had brutalised them and not given an inch. She wasn't expecting any mercy from him now. She knew he was thinking about how to kill her rather than what she could do to preserve her life. The sick fuck had zero poker face, but his actions throughout the day had already told her the answer. She wondered why she even pleaded in that manner. Just felt like the thing to say under the circumstances.

He clutched the pitchfork in his hand a little tighter. An idea had formed in his devious sadistic mind. This little bitch was going to get it worse of all, he told himself as he tilted his head down at her.

"Anything huh?" he repeated to Whitney in his triumphant atrocious drawl.

She had kept eye contact with him throughout his daydreaming and could now see his sinister smile twisting even further. Whatever he had planned wasn't going to be pleasant. He was going to kill her, just as she had thought, but at this moment she welcomed death. Welcomed the escape from his torture, from this seemingly endless day that had taken the lives of her friends and would now take hers too.

But she knew she didn't want to die. If there was a way out of this she'd take it no matter what nasty shit he had in store for her. She wanted to escape this day by any means necessary, but if she could escape it with her life intact then all the better, despite whatever nightmares would undoubtedly follow her for the rest of her life.

"Lick my pitchfork," he finally sneered with all his nauseating black and yellow teeth on full display. He grabbed the back of Whitney's head and wrapped his fingers around her blood-soaked blonde hair dragging out this last moment and making sure she knew he had all the power right to the end.

Before he could pull Whitney's head forward on to the spikes of the pitchfork and get his latest thrill, a different farming tool landed a blow. Standing behind him Abby unleashed a furious swing of her spade to the back of Psycho Hillbilly's head. He dropped to the muddy ground without the slightest clue what had happened. He was all ready to jam that bitch's head on to his pitchfork after delivering his awesome innuendo and watch it pierce her skull and pop her fucking eyeballs out and then suddenly he was out cold. What a waste, he would have thought if he was still conscious.

Whitney had closed her eyes when he grabbed the back off her head. She knew this was the end. The last thing she had seen was the pointy end of the pitchfork and the sharpness glaring back at her. She had felt the force of his hand readying to skew her. Her life hadn't flashed before her eyes, nor did she take a nostalgic trip back to the good times, she had just simply accepted this was the end. But it wasn't.

She looked up and saw someone else standing in the place that Psycho Hillbilly had occupied. Abby. Her eyes drifted to the ground where Psycho Hillbilly laid unconscious, pitchfork at his side and lacking her head which was still very much attached to her own shoulders. She hadn't felt his grip release from her head, nor his fingers unravel from her hair. She hadn't heard the sickening flat sound of the spade connecting with the Psycho Hillbilly's head. For a brief moment her mind had drifted to nowhere, but it wasn't hiding anymore.

"Thank you! Thank you! Thank you!" Poured out of Whitney's mouth when she finally put together what had happened. With some energy suddenly flowing back into her she leapt to her feet and into Abby's arms, grateful to her saviour.

Abby hadn't really noticed Whitney's show of gratitude. She

was busy looking around once again for someone to yell cut, or for a doctor to run on set and help Psycho Hillbilly. But just as with Swamp Boy nothing happened. Psycho Hillbilly remained out cold and nobody else was around to witness or stop any of it.

Tears flowed from Whitney's stressed face but for the first time all day they were happy tears rather than distraught ones. She was near delirious at the thought of still being alive after accepting her fate. Her whole body was trembling. Abby's first thought at noticing Whitney in her arms was that this wasn't the bad acting she'd seen in the film, this reaction was real. Abby had just genuinely saved this poor girl's life. But that just brought more questions than answers. Abby couldn't help but tenderly embrace the grateful girl despite those mounting questions.

She couldn't remember the last time she held someone in her arms. Abby didn't have any little nieces or nephews, no little cousins or anything like that. None of her friends had kids and she was quite limited on friends anyway. The ones she did have, she didn't hug any of them as a greeting or goodbye. It was safe to say Abby wasn't a hugger. She hadn't had a relationship in a while, and that hadn't really consisted of much affection anyway. She regretted that but would never have told him. Abby, as mentioned, just wasn't a people person. That, however didn't mean she didn't care. She cared a great deal about people, she just generally didn't want to spend any time with them.

But she couldn't help but embrace this poor beaten down broken girl. This girl that absolutely needed a hug after a horrific day. She could feel the tears pouring from Whitney's face getting her shoulder wet, but Abby didn't mind. She could feel Whitney's heart racing as her warm trembling body was glued to Abby's. Her arms were wrapped around Abby in a manner that suggested she'd never ever let go. Abby would grow tired of that pretty quickly under normal circumstances but didn't mind it for the moment as she'd been having a pretty crazy fucking evening herself. She felt an instant need to protect Whitney from any other evil, she'd been through enough, as Abby could attest to being somewhat of an unknowing bystander to it all.

Abby's own tears began to form as she surveyed her surroundings. This is all real she thought. This is all happening. She looked at the horrified girl in her arms. Stared at the ominous farming boneyard that lay in front of her. Studied the creepy battered farmhouse that stood behind her. Gawked at the terrifying Hillbilly Mom who had emerged from the dilapidated house full of anger and rage and was making a beeline for the pig pen they currently stood in.

That kicked Abby back into gear as she watched Hillbilly Mom stomping towards them. She was ready to tell Whitney it was time to go when Psycho Hillbilly grabbed her leg from his downed position. Abby tried kicking him away but he had a good grip. How many creepy fucking things had grabbed her today was beyond ridiculous. She had faced every terror imaginable in one evening and still didn't understand why, or just how much danger she was truly in. Just that they relentlessly kept coming and all seemed to want to grab her, kill her, or do something even worse.

He smiled up at her with his alternating black and yellow teeth showing like he just caught the catch of the day. The smile didn't last long however as this time Whitney brought the spade down hard and knocked him the fuck out. Psycho Hillbilly let go as Whitney went to town on him repeatedly bringing the spade up and back down. She didn't have much to her and barely had the energy to stand so the force wasn't that great, but it was still metal on skull and metal won every time as she bashed him again and again.

Abby joined in the fun giving him a few kicks now that her leg was free as Whitney continued the beat down. Hillbilly Mom came closer into view and saw the assault for herself.

"You whores get off my son," she screeched and began to move quickly towards the pair with a massive rolling pin in her hand and a shotgun that looked more like a canon strapped to her back.

Abby stared at her uncertain what to do, but Whitney knew. She took Abby's hand and led her out of the pig pen as the pair made their way towards the boneyard. Psycho Hillbilly lay in the mud having had the living shit beaten out of him, but he was still alive. Pain shot all over his body, but his thirst for blood-soaked vengeance would soon return, once he regained consciousness.

Boneyard

Whitney began to blindly navigate Abby through an array of broken equipment within the farming boneyard. Old discarded troughs, rotten hog pen fencing, various wrecked tools, different twisted metals, along with several stripped-down vehicles all rested in the boneyard. Stacks of old worn tires rusted wheels, planks of wood, and metal sheeting filled in the gaps. A variable junkyard showing the history of the farm through its broken and ruined equipment. Why had the farm needed so many troughs? And how were they all so broken and rusty? How had all this fencing snapped and rotted down the years? How had all these vehicles got here and been stripped bare? Were they like that beforehand, or after? Did they belong to the farm, or as Abby more suspected did they belong to victims of Psycho Hillbilly? The boneyard held a lot of secrets but it was in no rush to reveal the answers.

As they moved deeper into the boneyard Abby caught sight of the truck she had spotted from afar. There were plenty of other vehicles surrounding Abby but they were all in parts and barely even qualified as vehicles anymore. No use to anyone, least not as a getaway car. The truck however stood proud, if not somewhat dirty and rusted itself. But it was the only vehicle that wasn't missing its wheels and didn't have its engine sitting next to it. This engine was in the right place as far as Abby could tell. The truck could be their way out of here.

Abby had once tried to learn how to drive. She had about six lessons and hated every single one of them. She reasoned that some people weren't meant to drive, and she was one of those people. She couldn't get the hang of it, sucked at it, and ultimately didn't see herself getting any better so naturally decided that she just didn't want to drive.

She was a clever girl, extremely smart in a lot of ways, so couldn't understand how any old meathead or bimbo could pick up driving easier than her. It had to be more about want than intellect. Clearly she must not have wanted it she decided, although that still didn't sit right with her. Abby wanted to blame the driving instructor too, and tried to at first, but in the end she had to admit the obvious. She just couldn't drive. Be it want or intelligence, or whatever else, she just couldn't do it. It was a particularly annoying period of her life but one that she'd mostly forgotten about with it ultimately not mattering and her finding no real reason to have to drive, until now.

Whitney either hadn't noticed the vehicle or wasn't thinking about it. She was still ploughing forward through the yard determined to put as much distance between herself and Psycho Hillbilly, or his equally scary mum, as she could. She was dragging Abby along with her which Abby hadn't fully realised until she saw the truck disappearing from sight. Abby wasn't normally one to be led anywhere, especially in a dangerous situation. She'd normally be the one to take charge, or have some kind of plan, but she hadn't at the time of need and Whitney had, so for the moment Whitney could lead the way.

Newly formed clouds began to drift across the impossibly bright moon that illuminated the boneyard. It was the first time all night that the moon hadn't dominated the sky and lit the area. The thick clouds slowly started to cut the light from the enormous moon bringing some much needed extra darkness on to the farm. The convenience of it seemed absurd. The sort of thing Abby would have booed at the screen for in a movie while no one else cared. They'd have not realised how convenient it was, what lazy storytelling it was. It's just the sort of thing the Splatploitation Brothers would pull. She hated that sort of storytelling, it always felt too manipulative to her, too contrived.

That said Abby often liked the use of weather to depict a

character's mood in her own scripts so maybe she was just more pissed off with the whole situation and needed to get over herself for a moment. It did feel very heavy handed however how quickly the moon sunk behind the clouds. But surely the Splatploitation Brothers couldn't control the weather as well? Or was Abby controlling it in a drug-filled dream her mind wondered again.

As if to further anger Abby cackles of thunder followed the sweeping darkness. But if she was completely honest with herself this convenience was well, convenient. It gave them more flexibility to hide and to cover their tracks, just like it was meant to in the movies when it added to the suspense of a scene. Another trope that grated Abby. But this wasn't a movie. This was life and death with a pair of crazy killers after them, so this wasn't the time to be feeding her pet hates. This was time to be more glass half full and accept the help of the all too convenient weather at the precise moment they needed it.

The awful shouts of Psycho Hillbilly and his mum reverberated behind them. Abby could make out a different swear word or two in between the increasing claps of thunder as the tone of their voices somehow got more incensed, if that was even possible. Lightening started to accompany the thunder but still no sight of any rain. Just a newfound darkness alongside thunder and lightning with a couple of psychos on the loose chasing some young girls. The scene has been set, Abby dryly thought despite the fear building inside her.

Whitney took a sharp turn to the left still tightly holding Abby's hand. It could have been to direct Abby through the labyrinth of junk, but it wasn't, it was for comfort. It was the need to have someone with her. Something to help her feel a little more safe after the horrific day she'd had. If they weren't being chased and navigating a maze of crap and instead where strolling through a park she'd still want to hold her hand. She just needed some warmth and kindness after the torture she had endured, along with the loss of her friends.

She hadn't had much time to think about those losses. She'd obviously had some thoughts run through her head when she first saw their bodies but hadn't had time to grieve. Whitney wanted to. She wanted to sit down and burst into tears right now. She wanted to explode with emotion and cry forever at the loss of those closest to her, but she couldn't. This horrendous fucking day wasn't over yet and her wails and cries would only attract the attention of those psycho fucks. She caught a much-needed break in Abby saving her, but now wasn't the time to celebrate and mourn her losses, now was the time to escape for good.

Whitney led them to the large creepy barn Abby noticed when she first arrived at Hillbilly Farm. Up close it looked even more menacing which considering it already looked pretty fucking shady to begin with didn't fill Abby with joy. Planks of wood hung loosely from the roof and doorway with oversize nails baring their sharpness with evil intent. Filth and blood were spread across the dirt that led towards the entrance. Dead birds were still perfectly perched in the various holes within the crumbling wooden structure. Twisted wire was wrapped around different parts of the exterior without rhyme or reason. Even a small pile of hay running the length of the barn entrance looked beyond dirty. Like you could catch something just by stepping on it.

There were symbols drawn on to the outside of the barn as well. Not noticeable at first, but the closer the girls got the more they stuck out. What the symbols were for wasn't clear, but they definitely added to the overall sinister nature of the barn, which incidentally was actually their exact purpose. This was easily the least inviting barn anyone could ever come across. It screamed come inside me and get fucking tortured, raped, murdered and ripped in half while your organs are fed to demons. If Abby had to draw the most evil, nasty, forbidding barn she could possibly think off, it would look exactly like this. And Whitney wanted them to go inside? Fuck that!

Abby stopped. Her normal logical senses had returned. No fucking way was this a good idea and she knew it.

"We've got to hide," Whitney desperately pleaded motioning towards the sinister barn.

"We're not hiding in that creepy ass death trap," Abby curtly replied with the vigour she normally reserved for her roommate.

"But...." Whitney replied before getting cut off.

"Not a chance."

Whitney looked around the boneyard as the pair heard several more shouts echo behind them. Psycho Hillbilly and his mom drew nearer. Both accents really were the worst, like fingers down a chalkboard bad. How did they ever pick up such a foul way of talking? Surely it wasn't naturally. It sounded fake, but the accents weren't slipping. Every time the girls heard them they spoke in the same vile drawl. The thunder was still helping disguise their own conversation, but somehow Psycho Hillbilly and his mum rose above that. Turned out that nauseating accent did have its advantages.

"We could double back to the house," Whitney suggested without really thinking. No fucking way would she ever step foot in that house again.

"Are you trying to get yourself horribly killed?" Abby bluntly replied.

The nasty shouts behind them were getting a lot closer now. Shadows from the pair were moving in and the girls weren't exactly hiding, more just standing in front of a creepy barn waiting to be caught. Abby's hang ups of what waited for them inside wouldn't matter soon if they stayed out in the open like this.

Abby took Whitney's hand this time and led her away from the barn and the cruel shouts. The pair ducked under a broken tractor and crawled beneath its wheels away from the remaining light and into complete darkness. From their vantage point they could see a little in front of them but anyone looking towards the tractor wouldn't spot them in the shadows as long as they kept quiet and didn't move too much. They were far enough away from the barn for it to be partially out of sight but its presence still loomed.

"No place to hide girlies. I'll have you both on my barbie by the morning," Psycho Hillbilly taunted with a gleeful tone. Apparently fully recovered from his beat down he was now enjoying this extra little cat and mouse time he was getting with Whitney despite previously looking forward to executing her. They kept quiet as his boots appeared in front of them. It seemed to both like he had found them, but luckily he hadn't. He had just stopped to try and be sneakier. To creep around more quietly than he previously had, despite just shouting out seconds beforehand. He was an idiot Abby concluded, but a very dangerous one.

Whitney kept her hand over her mouth the whole time he slowly trod past. She didn't dare to even take a breath. This was the first time all day she had actually got away from him. The few times she'd got away previously he was a couple of steps behind and she still in his full view. This time was different. For once he didn't know where she was and she had no intention of him finding out. Abby too stayed perfectly still, but her brain was still trying to work out what the hell was happening.

Abby and Whitney

Psycho Hillbilly passed without noticing them under the tractor, but he didn't stray too far. He continued his search around the boneyard occasionally shouting out some abusive threat while his mom did the same. The rain still hadn't come but the thunder and lightning were fiercer than before. Even those awful drones from the pair were starting to finally be somewhat washed out. Not enough for Abby and Whitney not to hear them, but that wasn't a bad thing. Despite the language being fucking despicable it did at least allow the girls to keep track of the slashers whereabouts.

The pair stayed where they were talking in hushed tones. Whitney had shook Abby's hand as she introduced herself but Abby already knew who she was. Abby didn't let on she knew, but only because she still wasn't sure what was happening. Whitney had a little colour return to her face as she lay flat on the floor alongside Abby. She was excited to make a new friend, despite the extreme circumstances.

"Do you have a plan?" Whitney asked all out of ideas herself. Not that running into the boneyard was an idea to begin with, but it seemed better than being caught, beaten, and shot by Hillbilly Mom.

"Working on it," Abby replied with an idea starting to form. The trouble with any plan was she still didn't have a clue what was going on. But for the moment she figured any plan that kept them alive and out of the clutches of Psycho Hillbilly and his deranged mom was a half decent one.

"Do you know how far the main road is from here?" Abby quietly asked thinking whether the truck really could be their ticket out of here.

"I don't know where here is," Whitney replied in an almost

embarrassed way, not that she had to be. Abby didn't know either.

"Do you know anything about this place?" Abby asked hoping that together they could work it out.

"Not really," Whitney replied after a short deliberation. "I didn't know about this junkyard," she stated tilting her head a little to partially look around it from their hiding spot. "I was trapped in the house, and then escaped to the pig pen, but everything else is kind of missing." She thought about it a little more, baffled by her own statement. "I didn't even remember how I got here," she added.

Abby gave her a reassuring rub on the shoulder as she could see tears beginning to form once again in Whitney's eyes. Abby wasn't one for affection but she'd probably shown Whitney more care in the last ten minutes than anyone else in the previous couple of years of her life. She couldn't shake the guilty feeling she had of having witnessed a lot of Whitney's torment despite not really understanding what that meant as it was all in film form at the time.

"I remember being at a beach, but it wasn't any better there," Whitney said with a sadness in her voice. Like she'd already lived through this. "We were attacked there too," she added in a confused afterthought as though she didn't quite know what to make of that information. She was struggling to piece any of this together. "But that was by someone else I think." She looked to Abby as Abby kept watch. "Weird right. What are the odds?"

Abby's head snapped towards Whitney taking a really good look at her for the first time. She hadn't really paid much attention when they first meet as she'd seen her in the film not long ago, but now there was something familiar about her.

"God, that was you wasn't it?" Abby asked almost excitedly like she had solved a piece of the puzzle while skimming over the attacked there too part.

Whitney looked back at Abby confused, clearly not in on the revelation.

"You're an actress," Abby enthusiastically added.

Abby was starting to remember the girl in front of her from another Splatploitation Brother movie. She hadn't really noticed it was the same actress at first as they always just seemed disposable and interchangeable in the Splatploitation Brothers produced movies. There was no point noticing them because you were never going to get depth, or a good performance, just blood and tits. So Abby barely took note as to who any of them were. But she could see it now. This was the actress from their last abomination, *Gore Girls of Slasher Beach*. She was abysmal in that too, but Abby kept that to herself. What a piece of shit that film was thought Abby while remembering the scathing review she gave it. In retrospect that had probably contributed to the Splatploitation Brothers coming after her. She really had relentlessly slaughtered their films over the years.

"I am," Whitney said proudly interrupting Abby's daydream and happy to be recognised. "What have you seen me in?"

"This," Abby abruptly replied forgetting about that last piece of garbage film for a moment.

"This?"

"This whole thing. I've seen this farm. I've seen that Psycho Hillbilly fuck. I've seen him kill your friends. Kill you. I've seen it all in the last film you were in."

"Oh," Whitney replied, "so I have been here before?"

Whitney suspected she had. She was wondering why she remembered the farmhouse so vividly. Why the pigpen seemed familiar. She hadn't recognised the boneyard when she entered it but that was because she'd never been in there before. She still couldn't remember seeing it before despite it being close to the pigpen, but then she had had other things on her mind at the time, like crawling around in pig shit and being spiked in the face with a pitchfork. So many memories seemed on the edge of Whitney's mind but things were still hazy. She wasn't sure why, and this wasn't the time to be trying to figure it out.

It was Abby's turn to be confused.

"What's going on?" She asked hoping that she might finally get the answers she craved. "If you know anything about where we are," Abby added desperate for Whitney to spread some light on what the fuck had been going on.

Before Whitney could offer any answers Psycho Hillbilly circled round again. His thick heavy muddy boots sunk into the ground as he stomped around the boneyard. His footsteps seemed angrier than before, like he was running out of patience, which he was. At first he had enjoyed the extra chase, but now he was ready for the kill again.

"Where the fuck are you?" He roared unimpressed with their stunning hide and seek abilities. The thunder had finally started to die down and his awful drawl was dominating the air once more. His words would have been clear as day to the girls if it wasn't for his hideous accent.

"You're only making it worse for yourself," he lied. It was already going to be the worse experience imaginable for both of them when he got his mitts around their necks. That hadn't changed from the second they beat the fuck out of him. They weren't making anything worse, just delaying the horrors. The moment that spade connected a quick death was no longer on the table. He was the sort of guy to hold a grudge, especially when that grudge was his supposed victims getting the better of him. How dare they? This was his playground, not theirs.

He veered away from their hiding spot. Both Whitney and Abby kept a close eye on his movements and followed every step. Neither made a sound despite both being eager to carry on the conversation. Abby wanted answers, and Whitney wanted help trying to piece things together. They got their chance soon enough as Psycho Hillbilly disappeared out of sight. He seemed to be heading towards the back end of the boneyard where his sadistic mother was searching for them judging by their loud shouts to one another. The word, "whore," was used an unrealistic amount of times which had Abby shaking her head, but then what do you expect from someone who kills and eats people.

"What's the last thing you remember?" Whitney asked in a whisper regaining Abby's attention.

"I remember being at university, editing. Then these complete dicks that call themselves the Splat…"

"Splatploitation Bothers aimed a camera at you!" Whitney enthusiastically interrupted keen to show she did have some idea what was going on.

Abby nodded. So it was the camera she thought. Finally, something to go on, although it still didn't make any sense to her.

What did the camera have to do with all of this? Her first thoughts had always been that they were making some kind of film, and she'd stuck to the theory despite it not really making sense. Had they kidnapped a bunch of people for this film? Had the exact same thing happened to Whitney? Although, she'd been in some of their films before, so was she in on it? Abby took a quick suspicious glance at Whitney. She knew right away this girl wasn't in on whatever was happening. She wasn't that good of an actress as her two previous roles confirmed.

"Although I was at a club not uni," Whitney added to break the weird silence that had drifted into the conversation while Abby thought about the significance of the camera.

"I don't get it," Abby said aloud pondering the new information but unsure what it meant.

"Well I'm not clever enough to go to uni," Whitney blurted out once again without a second thought.

"No shit," Abby rudely replied even in their current situation. "That's not the part I don't get."

"Oh! The camera," Whitney finally replied taking an eternity in Abby's mind to catch on.

"Yes. The camera."

Whitney shook her head. "Me neither."

"Useful. So once again where are we?" Abby asked knowing that she wasn't going to get a good answer from Whitney.

But before Whitney could answer Psycho Hillbilly leaned under the tractor grinning ear to ear as he stared directly at the girls. His southern drawl was gone as he answered the girls, it sounded normal for once, familiar, but neither noticed or were thinking that at the time.

"You're in our world now," Psycho Hillbilly joyfully announced sounding exactly like Matthew.

The Truck

Abby instantly wiped the grin off Psycho Hillbilly's smug face with a sharp punch. She hadn't thought about it, as she had no clue that he'd spring himself on them like that, it just happened. Pure instinct. Abby had never been physically violent in her whole life prior to this evening. But she was a logical person, and much like with the Splatploitation Brothers earlier, sometimes you just had to do what needed to be done, and what had to be done here was to punch that sadistic asshole in the face. So that's what she did.

Psycho Hillbilly jerked back from his knelt position more out of surprise than anything else. The weak punch had barely grazed him but the jerk upwards had resulted in him banging his head on a set of unforgiving solid metal tractor steps hanging above the wheel. The little sting on his nose was nothing compared to the lump atop his head from the steel steps.

"You fucking bitch," he howled unaware that Abby and Whitney had already crawled out from under the tractor. They were not waiting around for him to try and grab them again and Abby had already hurt her hand on his face once and didn't really fancy a second punch.

It was the second time she had hit Matthew that night but in two very different incarcerations. She didn't think twice about kicking that dweeb in the nuts and dropping him to the floor, she almost found his rolling around in agony while crying funny but hitting Psycho Hillbilly was different. He seemed sterner, stronger. Hitting him hurt her. Abby's fingers ached and she might have twisted her wrist. It was just an altogether different experience on the same but not the same person. Definitely a confusing night in every possible way.

Abby guided Whitney between a host of ominous-looking broken vehicles trying to avoid the jagged metal parts sticking out from every direction. It felt as if someone had purposefully pulled all the doors and frameworks upwards and outwards to make the boneyard even more difficult and dangerous to navigate. Whitney caught her side on a damaged corroded metal door from an old car that would have served no purpose on the farm. She ignored the pain as it was nothing compared to what she had endured already that night, but it did hurt, and probably would require a shot judging by the state of the door.

Hillbilly Mom caught sight of her son holding his nose and the top of his head at the same time. With the nose being the least damaged of the two he used that hand to wave in the direction he thought the girls had taken off in.

"Pull yourself together," she barked at him. "It's just a couple of stupid little girls," she added with an extra venomous bite. She wasn't one to berate her son but normally she didn't need to. She was growing tired of these two little whores and wanted them in her oven sooner rather than later and wasn't used to her son fucking up. He was normally such a brutally adept Psycho Hillbilly slasher who never let his victims get any kind of win, let alone give them the possibility of escaping.

She had never been a patient woman and didn't enjoy the thrill of the chase the way her son did. She was a lot more efficient about things. The part she enjoyed was ripping them apart and being covered in their blood as their screams turn into everlasting silence. That was her thrill. None of this cat and mouse bullshit. None of this stalk them half the night to create more fear. She didn't care if they were afraid of her or not because she didn't feed on fear. She quite literally fed on flesh. In short, she just wanted to fucking eat them.

Psycho Hillbilly wanted to say something back, but he didn't. It wasn't because he didn't want to backchat his cannibalistic mom, he didn't care about that, the two argued plenty, it was because she was right. What the fuck was he playing at? They were just a couple of girls. Hell, he'd killed four that day and could have added Whitney to the body count a number of times, and that was a light day. He had days where he would kill a coach load before dinner. He had grown tired of them escaping him despite trying to persuade himself he was happy with an extra chase. Psycho Hillbilly was pissed. He had been shown up, humiliated. He'd let his mom down, and that was not fucking acceptable. They had to die, and painfully. He'd make her proud. Plus killing helpless annoying terrified girls was his favourite pastime anyway, so all the more reason to just actually do it.

Abby continued to lead the way as Whitney fell behind. The long day really had taken its toll and she was struggling to catch her breath. She already had a stitch on one side of her stomach and the car door had struck the other. In any other situation, she would have stopped for a breather already, but that simply wasn't an option. She willed herself to continue even if it was at a slower pace. Her stomach felt ready to burst and she could once again feel the tears forming, but she had to carry on. Abby gestured her to hurry up as they rounded another wrecked car. Whitney tried to fight through the pain and follow, getting the feeling that Abby had some kind of plan to get them out of here. That was definitely worth the extra push, but she really was moving on adrenaline alone.

Hillbilly Mom grabbed her rolling pin tighter than ever. The need to bash someone's fucking brains in with it was strong. She was in the mood for some ultra-violence and knew exactly who she wanted to take that out on. Those girls had evaded them long enough. She thought she caught a brief glimpse of Whitney in between some derelict cars but it could have been the shadows playing tricks on her. She headed in that direction anyway while her son circled round from the other side. They couldn't run from them forever.

"Can you drive?" Abby asked Whitney as she eyed up the pick-up truck twenty metres ahead of them.

"Got my provisional," Whitney replied sceptically.

Abby ignored the doubt in Whitney's voice. "Good enough."

Abby broke out into a sprint towards the truck. Whitney followed but slower. She was quick by nature, had always won the sprints at sports day, but she was in no real condition to run anymore this evening, or even walk for that matter despite their current predicament.

Whitney tried the door of the old truck as she arrived beside it while Abby began to work out if the engine was actually where it should be and not lying on the floor behind the beast of a truck. The hood was bent out of shape but beneath it as far as Abby could tell was an engine. Not that she knew anything about engines, but she did know that's where it was meant to be. Now it just had to work.

Abby hopped into the passenger seat after climbing a single step to get into the truck. The truck was a lot bigger than she first thought. Abby wasn't sure if that was an advantage or not. It certainly offered a lot of protection, but it wasn't in great shape. Whitney sat staring at the ignition.

"Do you have the keys?" She asked Abby knowing the answer had to be no.

Abby just smiled and checked the sun visor above Whitney. Sure enough, the keys were there strapped in via an elasticated band around them.

"How did you...?" Whitney started to ask but lost her train of thought in Abby's knowing smile. Whitney jammed the key into the ignition.

"Are we really in their world?" Abby asked still mauling over Psycho Hillbilly's statement. She had assumed it was a factual statement rather than just a one-liner because it actually made a lot of sense. Especially within the context of the farm. She obviously wasn't sure how, or even what exactly that meant, but the feeling in her gut told her that he was telling the truth. That it was a factual brag meant to make them feel helpless. While it did make Abby feel somewhat helpless she'd decided it helped more than it hindered as it did give her something to work with in unravelling the mystery of where she was and what had happened.

"I think so," Whitney replied almost like she was sure they were. The regret in her tone backed up that it was more than a 'think so.' She fully believed they were, but just didn't want to accept it.

"This makes no sense whatsoever," Abby stated, but for the first time began to think she finally had some answers no matter how crazy they were.

Both girls buckled up as Abby gave the nod for them to get the hell out of here. Whitney fired up the truck and to her great surprise it started, albeit with a choke and a splutter. Whitney flicked the headlights on ready to make a move but the truck instantly stalled. Whatever good luck they had in the thing actually starting hadn't lasted long. Whitney cursed as she tried to start the truck up again. Abby watched Whitney frantically turning the ignition as she caught sight of Hillbilly Mom stamping towards them. She still had the rolling pin held tightly in her hand but not for long. She slid the pin into her apron despite it being covered in nails and pulled out the cannon-like shotgun from her back.

"Fuck," was all Abby could say when Hillbilly Mom took aim and shot the ridiculously big looking shotgun-come-cannon in their direction.

The truck jolted forward just in time to miss the bulk of the blast. The shot had connected with the back end of the pick-up but it hadn't stopped them being able to drive away. Whitney slammed her foot down hard as she caught sight of Hillbilly Mom reloading the cannon shotgun. Another blast headed in their direction but the truck was moving too fast by that point as Whitney swung the vehicle precariously around a broken tractor that caught the brunt of the discharge.

Whitney could feel the back end of the truck dragging its heels. While they had escaped the first blast and it hadn't stopped the truck from working, it had caused plenty of damage. The cargo bed was missing a side and the whole back end of the truck was drooping. It wasn't quite touching the floor and Whitney still had control, but it felt like the pick-up could just fall apart at any moment. The tractor that took the second shot was a good example of what would have happened if the shot connected properly. The front of the tractor was fucked. Not that it wasn't already, but the loose framework it did have was no more. The shotgun had practically disintegrated it, and if anyone was inside it was certain they'd have ceased to exist too.

Through the missing doors of another ruined car, they saw Hillbilly Mom drop the shotgun to the floor. Out of bullets. She took out her rolling pin once more and continued her pursuit taking an easier route than the truck could manage through the boneyard. She was starting to look rather spritely for a near hundred-year-old woman clearly energised by the close call of nearly blowing the girls in half. They could practically see her wicked smile. In truth, she was just even more pissed off that they were still alive and that the shotgun hadn't destroyed them. How could she scold her son when she too had let them escape?

Whitney's sigh of relief at the gun no longer being in play didn't last long as she caught sight of Psycho Hillbilly waiting in front of them. He stood dead ahead of the truck with his pitchforked poised tightly in his hand like he was some kind of Spartan warrior. A sadistic smile once again spread across his face at the delight of finding the girls. The smile didn't last long.

Before Abby had a chance to suggest it Whitney floored the truck. It hurtled forward accelerating towards him. The grin had already faded by the time the pick-up splatted him against the deck and he disappeared under the wheels. Whatever his plan was when he confronted the truck, it hadn't worked. Whitney didn't give mowing him down a second thought. She almost looked excited at having the opportunity to make that Psycho Hillbilly fuck roadkill. Abby couldn't blame her, she felt exactly the same. In fact, she was kind of disappointed she wasn't the one behind the wheel running the cunt over.

But their win was short-lived as the bump from running down Psycho Hillbilly, along with the already sorry state of the truck, made Whitney lose control of the steering. Before she could regain control they were heading straight towards the creepy nightmarish barn that seemed to be welcoming them with open arms.

The Barn

The doors to the barn flung open as the rugged truck rammed through them. They were long past their prime like most things on the farm, and this was quite a spectacular way for them to have their final moment. Both of the decaying doors hit the floor already snapped in half after being run through by the merciless truck that seemed to be claiming all types of victims. Just like that it was now an open barn rather than one hiding behind closed doors, but that didn't make the place any less unsettling.

The truck came to a screeching halt inside the dark barn inches away from an unidentified machine. Remnants from the wooden doors stuck from the truck's grill and spiked the machine, but its attack was short-lived as the front of the pick-up dropped to the deck. The barn doors had also managed to twist the hood of the truck upwards even further, but like the underside, the hood also fell to the floor. The truck now looked like all the other wreckages scattering the boneyard. They may not have been the most sturdy of doors against the big truck but the pick-up was far from its prime and the deceased doors really had held their own by taking the truck down with them.

Smoke started to slowly drift from the engine that had miraculously stayed in place while everything around it came apart. Not the sort of smoke that was going to make the truck suddenly burst into flames and explode right there and then, but more the type of smoke that indicated it had had enough. The engine was done for, tapped out. It barely had any life to begin with, let alone after the excitement of the last few minutes. Being shot at, mowing down its owner, then destroying the barn doors had proved too much. In defence of the engine, the truck was done for whether it was smoking or not considering half the front of the pick-up was already lying prone on the barn floor.

The girls were jolted forward in their seats upon the initial collision, but both were glad they had instinctively put their seatbelts on during their failed getaway. They'd survived the crash.

"Weren't we trying to avoid the creepy barn," Abby said in jest, trying to lighten the mood after Whitney had potentially just killed a man and wrecked his property, not that he didn't deserve it. Abby cranked her neck a little to check it was ok and luckily it was. She didn't notice any new injuries and almost laughed considering the way they had mounted up throughout the night.

Whitney however had added to the bruise list with a giant one now covering her left shoulder spreading either side of her bikini strap where the seatbelt was. The strap had stopped her flying through the window, but apparently that was a compromise. Not that Whitney cared, for her it was just another bruise. One of many that had made a home on her body that evening.

"It's even creepier inside," Whitney muttered staring forward at the silhouettes of a bunch of machines directly in front of the wrecked pick-up. Everything beyond and to the side of the front machines remained engulfed in darkness and a mystery to the girls. There did appear to be some hooks hanging from the ceiling within eyeshot, but neither of them noticed. Abby gave Whitney a no-shit look in reply to her statement as she carefully unbuckled her seatbelt. It really did look even more sinister on the inside and that was before they could really see that much of the place. Only going to get worse, they both thought.

"Did I kill him?" Whitney asked with hesitation in her voice. She wasn't sure what side of the hesitation she landed on. The side where she had just taken a man's life, evil or not that was still a lot to process. Or the side where he had survived and would be shortly stalking them again. She couldn't take being hunted and tortured anymore so was hoping he was dead, but she didn't like having those types of feelings. When she saw Psycho Hillbilly standing in the way, him living or dying hadn't overly crossed her mind, she just wanted to run the fucker over and get the hell out of there. But still being on the farm meant that she'd probably find out one way or another whether he was dead or alive. She really would have preferred to escape and live in ignorance as to the result of her purposeful hit and run.

"Hopefully," Abby finally answered almost shouldering half the blame for Whitney. If the sole witness felt like she had done the right thing then maybe she had. After all that sick fuck had tried to kill her multiple times, massacred her friends, and chucked a fucking pig at her. He had it coming.

The pair climbed out of the truck. Abby somewhat gracefully jumped to the floor which was made easier by the pick-up tilting forward with the suspension broken and its guts all over the deck, while Whitney's descent was more of a fall. Her shoulder gave way as she used that arm to manoeuvre herself out of the truck. She tumbled lightly to the ground and wanted to stay there for a bit. Rest felt good, felt needed. Sure the barn was creepy as fuck but maybe a good night's sleep would help. She stared up at the still-smoking engine thinking maybe this close to the truck wasn't the best place for any rest though.

Abby circled the truck to help Whitney up and spotted the nasty bruise on her shoulder. Whitney assured Abby it was nothing, that it was just keeping all the other bruises she'd suffered throughout the day company. An anger rose up in Abby at hearing of the poor girl's hardship and seeing that Whitney wasn't joking. Even in the poor light of the barn, Abby could see that Whitney was covered in bruises, head to toe. It seemed almost impossible to Abby that Whitney could even move or talk at the moment having taken a proper look at the state of the girl.

"Could have been a lot worse if it wasn't for you saving me," Whitney offered in an attempt to set aside Abby's concerns. Abby barely heard the words as she continued to run her eyes over Whitney's beaten body.

Sure, Abby had seen most of Whitney's suffering herself, and even thought the girl deserved it while watching *Hillbilly Farm* and getting annoyed at her stupid decision-making and even worse acting, but this was different. This wasn't a dumb stereotype from a movie sitting in front of her, well it still kind of was, but more so this was a person. Some sweet girl who hadn't deserved to be put through any of this. Abby wondered again whether she'd seen some kind of snuff movie, but that didn't explain the girl living and breathing after she'd seen her die so horribly and cringeworthy on screen. Her fucking face had been split in half. That wasn't the sort of thing you just walked off ready for another take.

"What happened to you inside the house?" Abby tentatively asked Whitney. She wasn't sure if she wanted to hear the answer, or even whether it was right to ask the question, but the words just came out when she looked down at the battered and beaten girl. Whitney shook her head fighting back the tears. She half-smiled to Abby as a thank you for asking but she didn't want to answer the question and Abby recognised that.

"Then you did the right thing mowing down that asshole," Abby reassured her. Whitney nodded in agreement. He really did deserve it, they both thought.

While Whitney didn't answer the question she did think about it. What had happened inside the house? If she was completely honest with herself she wasn't sure. She had the emotion inside of her of being tortured, tormented, abused, but none of the memories. Had she locked them away already? Was that some kind of coping mechanism which very quickly and instinctively kicked in or was it something else.

She thought hard about that time and couldn't recall anything. She didn't know what Psycho Hillbilly had done, how he had done it, or what exactly she had been through. She just knew somehow that she had. Were the memories repressed? The first thing she could remember from inside the house was running down the stairs and trying to escape. There were bits before that, stuff with her and her friends, the initial attack, being dragged into the house alone. But the rest of what happened inside was blank. Unwritten was the description that immediately entered her head.

As she started to really, really think about the whole ordeal it occurred to Whitney this wasn't the first time this had happened on the farm. That memory, however, was too far in the back of her mind to access at the moment, let alone process. But something was eating away at her. These thoughts and memories were far too jumbled for Whitney's liking considering it at all happened within the last few hours and she knew a key ingredient was missing. She needed some time to really try and put it all together but now wasn't that time. Plus she was definitely worried about what some of the answers might mean. For once it was Whitney wondering what the fuck was going on giving Abby a brief break from all those notions.

Abby had left Whitney deep in thought and had made her way to the open barn entrance. The moon had been battling with the clouds as it tried to reassert its dominance over the night sky and appeared to be winning. Abby could see different parts of the boneyard slowly illuminating again as the moonlight broke through and started to do its thing. The moon itself seemed bigger than ever, like its previous enormous state wasn't enough. It was clearly overcompensating for something, but for what Abby didn't know.

As the clouds began to lose the fight and more light entered the farm Abby spotted a figure strutting towards them in the distance. Hillbilly Mom stomped forward practically snarling. She was foaming at the mouth with her face contorted with even more hatred than she already had if that was possible. How many levels of anger did this nasty vile woman have? She clutched the rolling pin in her hand and meant business. It was time to fucking brain someone.

She tapped the makeshift bat in her hand with the loose, sharp, probably infected, nails protruding from the rolling pin barely missing her fingers. Abby wondered whether she knew she was that close to sticking the nails straight through her hand but Hillbilly Mom didn't give a shit. She just wanted revenge. Horrible, nasty, blood-soaked, ultra-violent revenge.

Hillbilly Mom

Whitney stood at Abby's side as the pair watched Hillbilly Mom nearing the barn.

"You know any martial arts?" Abby asked Whitney hopefully.

"Nope."

"Boxing?"

"No."

"Anything?"

"I once scratched a guy's eyes out for grabbing my ass," Whitney offered.

"Literally?" Abby replied thinking maybe Whitney was tougher than she looked.

"Literally, he used both hands."

"No, did you literally scratch his eyes out?" Abby asked with a shake of her head. This girl was sweet and all but she really was pretty dumb in Abby's opinion.

"Ugh. No. Of course not!" Whitney said shocked at Abby even thinking it.

Abby shook her head with a little more vigour, more through disappointment than being judgemental that time. She really could have done with a badass eye scratcher at her side.

Hillbilly Mom was in near earshot of the girls. She looked to the broken doors laying on the floor with her fiery eyes and then back to the girls as if she was even more pissed off with them for destroying her property. In truth brutally killing her son by running him over with a pick-up truck was more than enough to have her want to break those bitches in half. She wanted to fuck them up a few times over and then chop them up and fucking eat them. That was their best-case scenario.

"You girls are going to fucking pay for running over my

baby boy," she spat out. "I'm going to rip your faces off. Going to eat your fucking eyeballs. Make necklaces out of your teeth. Chop you into tiny bits…" she continued. Her foul-mouthed threats weren't even close to being over as the returned colour to Whitney's face washed away, but Abby wasn't paying attention to the old hag.

Abby searched the nearby area of the barn. She spotted a branding iron perched against the side of a nearby machine. She didn't pay much attention to the machine itself but took the branding iron and weighted it in her hand. It would do. It wasn't the heaviest looking weapon but it didn't look flimsy either. Wouldn't be anyone's first choice but in a pinch it could definitely cause some damage. The girls both took a few steps back further into the barn as Hillbilly Mum closed right in.

"So if I've got this right, this world is fake?" Abby asked Whitney not sure of her own question but trying to make some kind of sense of things.

"Fake?" Whitney replied.

"Like, we're not in Kansas anymore?"

Whitney considered it "Oh. Like *Wizard of Oz*?" She gave it a little more thought while Abby waited impatiently for an answer. "I guess we're not," Whitney finally said. "Least I don't think we're in the world we know," she added sceptical of her own comments. "I think we're in their world, somehow."

That was good enough for Abby. She nodded her approval at Whitney's dubious assessment and marched forward to meet Hillbilly Mom at the entrance to the barn. Hillbilly Mom was still busy laying on the threats as Abby arrived.

"Going to feed your remains to my pigs. Going to make the tiny parts of you left suffer. Going to…"

WHACK.

* * *

Abby smashed the branding iron hard into Hillbilly Moms' face lifting her off her feet and crashing to the floor. She hit the ground hard with her few remaining teeth now missing. The spiked rolling pin fell from her hand and landed out of reach. Abby wasted no time mounting the old woman on the deck and raised the branding iron up once more. Whitney watched in horror as Abby continuously brought the branding iron up and down relentlessly battering the elderly woman's head. Hillbilly Mom lay underneath Abby absorbing every single blow as the iron connected with her face time and time again. Abby absolutely fucking annihilated her. Went medieval and wasn't about to stop. She kept swinging as chunks of flesh and facial parts flew all over the place.

"What the hell are you doing?" Whitney cried. "She's like a hundred years old."

Abby didn't give a shit. She'd had enough. Sure this had been a big night for Whitney but Abby had had her share of it too and wasn't in the mood to take anymore. If this wasn't real in some kind of sense that Abby still couldn't wrap her head around, then what she was doing now was fine, she reckoned. If this was some kind of fake something, then fuck it, why take any more abuse off of this old cow or anything else with fiendish intentions.

She continued the outright assault on the old woman. Her arms weren't close to tiring and she wasn't about to stop until she couldn't swing the iron anymore. It wasn't that long ago she'd seen this woman cooking a human being and encouraging her son to do God knows what to Whitney. She deserved no mercy in Abby's eyes, and if she did, Abby certainly wasn't going to be the one to offer it to her. Abby just wanted to destroy her, along with all her threats and nasty intentions. She wanted out of this fucking hell hole and as far as Abby could tell this evil old crone was the last obstacle.

"She was cooking your friends," Abby stated noticing that Whitney was still looking horrified at her actions. "And was definitely going to cook us," Abby added while unleashing a few more whacks for good measure. By this point however she was just hitting the floor beneath her. Hillbilly Mom's face was long gone, turned to paste at the hands of Abby and her branding iron.

She'd gone limp after the first couple of whacks. Despite being tough as hell and nastier than the Devil himself, she was in fact a very, very, very old woman. She could still dish out the punishment, but no way could she take it like she used too. Once upon a time she would have got up even from this vicious beatdown. But those days where long ago and now definitely wouldn't see the light of day again considering she was a stain on the barn floor.

Abby nonchalantly stood up from the headless corpse of the elderly woman she had mounted and proceeded to fucking destroy. She was covered head to toe in the cannibal's blood. Her arms and face were barely recognisable from a few minutes before. If Abby had felt some sympathy for the death of Swamp Boy earlier and regretted her decision somewhat to kick his struggling body into the swamp, she shared no such doubts about Hillbilly Mom.

She was pleased with her work. Pleased she stood up for herself, Whitney, and all the other victims of this evil piece of shit. This horrible woman had taken the life of plenty of teens. This disgusting hag who had cooked fuck knows how many people in her lifetime and enjoyed them as a meal. No, there was no regret this time. This bitch had it coming, Abby thought without an ounce of remorse knowing that given the chance Hillbilly Mom would have done exactly the same to her, if not worse. In fact, she had said as much seconds before Abby brained her.

She threw the branding iron to the ground and dusted her hands off like a job well done. Whitney's mouth was still open, her jaw still dropped at the sight of what had just happened.

"It's not real anyway," Abby said with a shake of her head in an attempt to comfort Whitney who looked ready to be sick. Despite all that she had seen today most of it was her witnessing the aftermath, not seeing the actual devastation itself.

"That's not quite what I meant," Whitney replied looking at the red paste on the deck that used to belong to one of her tormentors' head.

Abby turned to Whitney with plenty of thoughts and ideas running through her head. She wanted to get this straight. To finally have some idea as to what the fuck was happening and felt that Whitney probably knew more than she did.

"So let me get this straight," Abby began. "Those Splatploitation fucks pointed a camera at me, at us, and somehow we've ended up here," she stated like it was a fact but unsure how.

Whitney nodded. Correct.

"And here, as I far as I can tell, is their world," she gestured with inverted commas around the 'their world.'

Whitney nodded in agreement once more.

"Right," Abby said to herself like she'd made a breakthrough but still didn't get it.

"What's the not quite what you meant part?" Abby asked backtracking slightly after finally taking in what Whitney had said moments earlier.

"Well," Whitney said in a teeny manner that she often used but hadn't really shown much during the current bloodbath. "What I meant was that you and I are real right?" She asked hoping that Abby was in fact real and would agree with her.

"I'm real," Abby said with plenty of authority.

"So am I," Whitney said with a lot less certainty even though she hoped and believed it to be true.

"So my point is what if…" she gestured to the mess that used to be Hillbilly's Mom on the floor. "Is real too."

Abby considered Whitney's theory. She hadn't really thought about it but what she was saying did make some kind of sense. But surely no one really acted the way this woman did. In a film, sure, absolutely, definitely. But in real life, Abby liked to think not.

"I think she's a character or something," Abby finally answered. "I don't think she got into this world the same way we did," Abby added hoping her words were true and that wasn't a real person's brains stuck to the bottom of her shoes.

"If she was real I'd have felt bad for what I just did," Abby continued while looking at the old woman's headless body on the filthy barn floor feeling zero remorse.

Abby took a deep breath as she turned away from the corpse to face Whitney and asked what felt like an important question to her after Whitney's hesitation of whether she was real.

"Do you remember a life outside of this world? Your own life?"

Whitney considered the question for a second. It was again something she hadn't really had time to think about with everything else that had gone on. But she did remember more than the blood and torture of the farm.

"I was an actress" she offered. "And modelled part-time," she added with her voice fading a little like that was a long time ago. She wasn't entirely sure about her answer though. It seemed true, it was definitely what she remembered, but like other recent memories, it felt a little hazy.

"And you got sucked into this world while you were at a club?" Abby reaffirmed.

Whitney nodded. That sounded about right.

"Do you know how long ago that was?"

"Months." Whitney replied knowing it to be true. Fuck. She had literally just lost months of her life.

Abby closed her eyes at the thought. They had to get the fuck out of this world.

Splatploitation Studio

In the bowels of the old fire station known as the Splatploitation Brothers Studio was a basement where very few had ever entered. In fact, only four people had ever been down there in its current incarnation, the Splatploitation Brothers themselves. The reason for this was that unlike the rest of the studio the basement wasn't for film production as such, it was more for exhibiting. The oddly-arched-shaped basement housed a homemade cinema, not a very tall one, but more like one of those wide ones you'd find in the midst of a crammed capital city. The roof was lower at the sides but the middle was just tall enough for a decent-sized screen. All in all it was a good space for a private independent cinema, especially one with a maximum capacity of four.

A projector, with an old-fashioned editing table beside it, sat at the back end of the basement pointing forwards towards a make-shift cinema screen. When they had first envisioned the room, the Splatploitation Brothers had pictured some kind of giant 4k cinema screen as the showpiece of the room but in its place was a big white sheet that had come with said projector. It was a very nice sheet, clean and well stretched, perfect really for projecting films onto, but still, it wasn't quite what they had in mind. That said they had grown to love the presentation on the sheet. The way the films looked on it. It seemed whenever the Splatploitation Brothers tried to endorse some kind of modern technology they always found ways to fall back on the old grindhouse ways.

A small sound booth and a bunch of mics on a table were situated to one side of the screen. The mics were all labelled for different things and this area seemed to be more than just for sound recording despite an initial glance looking that way. The mics were more related to the cinema itself rather than production with labels like 'whole world', 'direct to character', and 'editing machine' stuck onto them. Strangely, there were no headphones either, and the soundboard was limited to very few dials and sliders. This wasn't a setup to create incredible soundscapes for some big box office movie, it would barely pass useful for a student film, but it had its purpose.

The other side of the cinema was filled with film canisters and prop tables with a mess of things stacked on them. Strips of film hung from the low ceiling darkroom style next to the canisters, while painted monster models and masks gathered on the top, and all around the prop table. All manner of horror posters circled the room depicting every sub-genre and budget you could think of. They were plastered against the wall in an overlapping fashion rather than the nicely framed ones in Abby's apartment. More akin to a music venue than a cinema.

The middle of the room had exactly four comfy chairs, evenly spread, all pointing towards the screen. The Splatploitation Brothers had made a very conscious decision to just have the four chairs. This was their private room, their bat cave. It wasn't somewhere where they'd show the public or investors their latest movie, not a screening room for others. This was their very own private cinema which wasn't even known to anyone else, let alone visited by them.

The chairs were where the Splatploitation Brothers had afforded themselves a little luxury. The comfy cinema chairs weren't brand new when they brought them, but they were the real deal. Second-hand VIP seats straight from a closed down multi-chain. They liked the irony of these chairs being from a big chain, a place that showed huge blockbuster movies compared to their little no budget indie flicks. It felt like a win over the man. It fulfilled their underdog voice they often felt they had when comparing their movies to those coming out of

Hollywood and the Studio system.

The four Splatploitation Brothers sat in the chairs dumfounded at what had just taken place in front of them. All four were looking up at the homemade cinema screen which had just shown the absolute annihilation of Hillbilly Mom. They had managed to keep hold of their buckets of popcorn and massive drinks, but their jaws had hit the floor at the relentless beatdown Abby had afforded the old woman. The Splatploitation Brothers continued to look at the screen, at the barely recognisable remains of Hillbilly Mom, and wonder what the fuck had just happened. This wasn't how things normally went.

Unbelievably the screen had a direct link to the world that Abby and Whitney occupied. The projector sent a real time viewing of the Splatploitation World as the group had dubbed it, onto the white sheet at the front of the cinema for their viewing pleasure. They sat there in their comfy chairs watching the events of the Splatploitation World unfold complete with edits and quality sound. They could see and hear the world perfectly from their viewing spot with the occupants unaware of their gazing. Well mostly unaware. Abby had shown signs of thinking they were there somehow but that appeared more out of paranoia and guesswork.

"Poor Hillbilly Mom," Duncan quietly said, breaking the long silence that had followed the savage assault.

"I didn't portray my character to be killed by some girl," Matthew followed with, putting way too much emphasis on the word girl. Spoken like he was a five year old. He hadn't really cared about Hillbilly Mom's destruction, she was just another character to him. But he was still in shock at Psycho Hillbilly himself being run down and made into roadkill by Whitney. He'd launched into a rant at the point Psycho Hillbilly disappeared under the pick-up wheels but was told to shut up as the group all waited for Hillbilly Mom to take the revenge which never ended up happening.

"I'm just disappointed we didn't get to see Whitney's tits this time," Roger spurted out with his normal joyful tone and lack of tact. For all his faults he genuinely wanted to be seen as a fun-loving laid back guy, and to some degree he was, but a level of inappropriateness always seemed to come with that. Everyone in the room nodded in agreement however. The group had decided long ago one of the big perks of making horror films was the standard horror convention of the terrified teens always finding a way to get their tits out. The group had happily, and proudly, continued that convention in their own big screen adventures.

"This wasn't my vision," Percy angrily shouted to the room with all thoughts of Whitney's tits disappearing from his mind. He stood from the comfort of the chair and began manically pacing the room. "The scream queen dying is part of what makes us different."

He began to stare at several of the gory horror posters plastered against the wall like they were speaking to him. Every single one of them showed some teen in peril with an ominous figure nearby. He lowered his eyes from the posters like he had somehow let them down, that he had lost his voice in some way.

"It's part of our horror convention. Our trademark," he mumbled to himself, but still loud enough for the others to hear. Abby and Whitney defeating Psycho Hillbilly and his mum was sacrilege in his eyes.

The Splatploitation Brothers flicks always had their heroine die. They often followed the rules to a point, but instead of the shy virgin turning the tables on the killer in the third act like most slasher and horror movies, they upped the brutality and torture. They made the normally innocent survivor get it worst of all. If her ditzy friends had suffered at the hands of whatever nasty element was causing chaos this time then the pure sinless girl next door type was going to get it a lot fucking worse. That was their thing. Tease the normal horror structure, and then twist it by screwing over the final girl.

It had been the framework for every single one of their films. Never in the history of the Splatploitation Brothers Studio had the final girl survived. She had to be brutally murdered in the most gory way possible often while being stripped naked, abused, or degraded in some fashion. The Splatploitation Brothers didn't exactly hate woman, other than Matthew who definitely had some fundamental dislike for them, they just they loved old school horror and in the horror they liked the pretty teens got tormented. That's just the way it was. So when it came to their own films they decided to take that one step further, much to Matthew's delight.

Their hardcore fans loved it, but the Splatploitation Brothers got plenty of hate for it too. All the normal woman-hater comments, victim blaming, promoting violence, stuff you'd expect from the keyboard warriors out there. But they didn't give a fuck about that. They weren't mainstream. Most of the people that felt that way had accidentally stumbled across one of their films and been offended by it. Or worse still, had only heard about it and hadn't even watched the film to begin with. But their true fans, they loved it. They loved that the Splatploitation Brothers always seemed to take things too far. That they went to an awkward uncomfortable cringeworthy place. They were legends in the eyes of their fans, at least that's what they told themselves.

So it was one hundred percent completely and utterly unacceptable that Abby had destroyed Hillbilly Mom and Whitney had cut down Psycho Hillbilly. Sure this wasn't the version of Hillbilly Farm which was out there for everyone to see, this was their own private cut, but the rules remained the same. They had to have their principles.

"Maybe we should add a monster," Duncan interjected to anyone who would listen, but no-one was. He had made his way to the film canisters and started to flick through them. All of the canisters had gaffer tape stuck on the outside with B-Movie horror titles or crazy monster names scrawled across them in thick marker.

While Percy pondered what to do next, Matthew took the opportunity to try to become the centre of attention, the way he always liked it. He still wasn't remotely happy at Whitney running over one of his masterpiece characters. He always felt a lasting connection to the characters he played and could never accept their demise, mostly because he never had to. He was used to winning.

"Psycho Hillbilly is meant to be unstoppable," he shouted. His voice was a mixture of anger and whining.

"He's a B-minus character at best," Roger replied not really thinking so but sensing the opportunity to wind Matthew up.

"He most certainly is not!" Matthew instantly snapped back, much to Roger's delight.

Duncan stopped on one of the canisters.

"What about a Vampire?" he suggested. No one answered.

"He was just stumbling around after them. He had no method, no stalking ability. Jason would have chopped them in half by now. Fuck! Jason's mum would have made quicker work of them than Psycho Hillbilly," Roger teased Matthew who always took the bait.

"Every slasher plays a form of hide and seek. It's what they do. You need cat and mouse to build tension," Matthew countered in a patronising manner.

Roger however wasn't one to get upset like Matthew and preferred to double down instead.

"Fuck tension. I want gory kills. Tension is overrated. You

can't go wrong with a good massacre."

"Psycho Hillbilly is capable of delivering gory deaths," Matthew whined back.

"Yeah if you're prepared to wait an entity for his mummy to help him. Fuck that."

Matthew started to get animated. He hated it when Roger pushed his buttons like this, worse so when he was aware he was doing it. But Matthew couldn't help it, he couldn't just drop it and move on. He didn't want to either. He was right about this and he knew it. Psycho Hillbilly is an awesome slasher, he told himself over and over in his head all while Roger stood there with a shit-eating grin on his face waiting for Matthew's next comeback so he could put it down and twist it into a lie. Sometimes Matthew really did fucking hate Roger's guts.

"What about a Mummy?" Duncan suggested. "Would be kind of ironic," he said to himself laughing at his own too soon joke. Maybe this time it was lucky no one was listening to him because that joke definitely would have bombed. Duncan thought about repeating the classic joke he had just unleashed on the room but knew there was no point. He was invisible to them when they were in this type of mood. Or any type of mood for that matter. He suddenly thought maybe the invisible man could do the trick and stop Abby, but he was bored of the idea before he had even finished dreaming it up. He wanted something big and scary to do the job, something visual.

"We didn't want him to be a machine. We wanted him to be resourceful," Matthew finally countered. He couldn't help but have a smug look on his face as he remembered Percy saying those exact words when they were going through the script together. He knew Roger wouldn't contradict Percy. Game, set, and match, Matthew muttered to himself hoping he got the sports reference correct as sports weren't exactly his wheelhouse.

"But he's not resourceful," Roger replied already grinning to himself as he followed with, "Maybe you played him wrong."

He barely got the words out while keeping a straight face before Matthew exploded. Arms waving, feet stamping, Matthew knew how to throw a tantrum. He even threw his popcorn the length of the room which for him was impressive. Roger loved every second of winding Matthew up. He'd put his arm around Matthew and stick up for him if anyone else did it, but when Roger himself got to do it, well that was one of his great joys in life.

"What about the way he threw a pig at her?" Matthew screamed back at Roger in a eureka moment.

"Did it kill her?" Roger smugly replied. "Did he decapitate her with a pig? Did it actually do any harm whatsoever?"

"That wasn't on the page. I'm the actor, not the…" Matthew stopped short of saying writer. The last thing he wanted was Percy in on this argument too. Sure, Percy was in deep thought about Abby's survival but he had bat-like hearing when it came to anyone questioning his writing or directing. Roger had stopped too and offered Matthew a ceasefire smile. Neither wanted to piss Percy off, especially when he was in this kind of mood.

"We could splice in a Pan-Croc," Duncan suggested clearly not taking the temperature of the room, although he did finally get Matthew's and Roger's attention.

"What the fuck is a Pan-Croc?" Matthew asked Duncan, annoyed at him for saying such a silly word.

"Only one of my greatest ever creations," Roger proudly joined in. "Half Panda, half crocodile, all terror," he said like reading the tagline of a forties monster movie. In reality, it was a film that Roger himself never got to make, but God! he wanted to make that film. He had big ideas for the Pan-Croc. Roger fully believed he could make it the next great monster like the

Wolfman, or Dracula, or something else from Universal's back catalogue. Sadly for Roger, the idea stayed just that, but he hadn't given up on it.

Matthew didn't know how to reply to the Pan-Croc suggestion but luckily didn't have to.

Roger looked to Percy for approval of the idea of putting a Pan-Croc into *Hillbilly Farm* but he wasn't going to get it.

"I'm not ruining the artistic integrity of *Hillbilly Farm* by randomly adding a Pan-Croc," Percy said in a calculated way. Before Roger could protest Percy made it clear why. He grabbed a film canister from the table Duncan stood by and headed towards the projector, or more precisely the old Steenbeck beside the projector. He took the film from the canister ready to splice it using the machine. It was still unclear how all of this worked, what magic or darkness was on display, but Percy seemed to know.

"Psycho Hillbilly is getting an upgrade," Percy announced, much to the delight of the group.

Slaughterhouse and Upgrades

The moon lost the brightness it had regained when huge dirty dark clouds swallowed it whole and sent the entire farm into complete darkness. Abby and Whitney stood in the barn entrance staring out into nothingness. Rumbles of thunder that seemed to shake the barn to its very core quickly followed. When the first lightning strike hit the ground ten metres from the girls the lights and power inside the barn instantly flicked on to reveal the barn's true nature.

Behind the girls stood a fully working Slaughterhouse. A narrow chute at the front of the barn lead to a maze of moving platforms, conveyor belts, metal grills, thin pipes, buzzing saws, whirling machines, and a fuck ton of left over blood and gore from whatever last took a trip through the abattoir. This place would not pass any food hygiene or health and safety inspection, but it didn't need to as everything and everyone killed here was eaten a few hundred metres away at the farmhouse. The pièce de résistance at the end of the oddly funhouse-looking abattoir setup was a huge metal square that stamped downwards obliterating anything resting underneath it. What its purpose might have been was completely unknown, but a pile of bones beside it suggested the sort of things it had been used for.

Both Abby and Whitney had turned at the same time when they heard the commotion of machines start directly behind them. While Abby's eyes rested on the funhouse of terror Whitney's drifted to the hanging hooks to the side. They came complete with dead animals, human corpses, and blood filled troughs waiting beneath them. Whitney struggled fto

176

comprehend the barn, while Abby was beginning to catch on to the shitty way this world worked.

Abby could have sworn the barn hadn't been like this when they arrived. It was yet another environment that had changed. Just like the pathway leading away from Swamp Boy. After she had killed him that exit had suddenly appeared like it had just been added to whatever narrative she was in. Now, moments after she had butchered Hillbilly Mom, the barn had transformed into some kind of Slaughterhouse. What was with these sudden additions and transformations?

Sure, they'd both seen the outline of machines when they had arrived here, but nothing like this. Just like she had seen some kind of opening at the swamp, but nothing like what she ended up walking down. Whatever was going on Abby was certain things were getting continuously changed along the way. There were continuity errors all over the place. It didn't really make sense to her, but neither did much else at this time. She knew she was right though.

"Well why the fuck wouldn't the barn really be a Slaughterhouse?" Abby sarcastically said aloud.

The second bolt of lightning sent all the machines into overdrive. The noise of metal on metal inside the barn became deafening. The saws buzzed quicker, the metal stamper slammed faster, and the whirling machines whirled quicker. The only thing that didn't change speed was the travelator. It stayed stay at the same steady rate to create the right amount of drama and suspense if required, rather than get the job done too quickly and anticlimactically.

The machines weren't the only thing the lightning strikes had turned on. The truck had powered up too and began to roll backwards narrowly missing the girls. Its newfound life was short-lived however as it hit a pile of metal wreckage at the front of the barn previously unnoticed, or maybe just hadn't been there. It caused the engine to drop right out of the vehicle and crash hard on the floor.

The pair looked at what had been their only previous means of escape as it now took the form of the rest of the wrecked vehicles in this godforsaken place. It didn't really matter what had turned the vehicle on to begin with, because that was already stupid enough in Abby's eyes, but whatever made it role backwards and have the engine fall out was just plain dumb. She was no mechanic but Abby was pretty certain none of what had just happened was possible. Whitney's thoughts echoed Abby's as she stared at the broken vehicle knowing their only quick form of escape was gone. Not that either thought the pick-up still worked anyway, but clearly someone wasn't taking any chances.

The lights began to flicker in the barn similar to how they had in the university hallway. It put Abby on edge, and she could see it was having the same effect on Whitney. Abby knew Whitney had got wherever here was via the camera too, but she hadn't known whether she got the whole light and sound show as well. Abby was half waiting for the colours to bleed from the walls and that awful droning sound to return but quickly realised this light flickering wasn't like the camera. This was something else. And not just a normal light flicker something else either, it seemed too staged for that. This was more like a bad ominous dangerous something else.

The third bolt of lightning stuck the farm but this one was more accurate than the previous two. The others hadn't hit anything, they had merely been for effect it seemed. Just a way to turn the barn lights and power on in a creative way. But this lightning strike had a purpose, had reason to be. The third lightning strike had accurately struck its target adjacent to the barn. Abby and Whitney watched as the body of Psycho Hillbilly briefly lit up within the strike before the farm once again fell back into pitch black.

The girls couldn't see the results of the strike, just who it had hit. If they could see they would have realised the strike had brought Psycho Hillbilly back to life. Psycho Hillbilly gasped for air as the lightning hit him. A wave of electricity shot through his body lighting up all his senses and started his heart beating once more. That cold black heart of his was once again pumping evil blood through his veins and he could feel it.

But the lightning had more than just bringing him back to life in mind. While still laying on the floor shaking uncontrollably at the sensation flowing through his body Psycho Hillbilly began to change. He began to grow taller first stretching from his previous height to nearer seven feet. Then his muscles began to slowly expand. What had previously been a somewhat scrawny frame was beefing up big time. He'd previously looked like some kind of evil malnourished farmhand but now he looked more like a wrestler, or a gladiator, albeit an ugly one. His muscles started to bulge and his neck thickened, the boils on his body began to grow too. Thick veins started to show throughout his arms and head but appeared black in colour. Whatever this transformation was it wasn't simply a growth spurt.

He could feel his biceps exploding with power, his legs expanding with strength. Even his overalls were starting to up a bunch of sizes without ripping too much. Rolls started to appear on the back of his head as his new form continued to grow. The shaking stopped as he took shape. He was more in control again despite the growth continuing. All he could think during the whole rebirth and transformation was fuck yeah, this is awesome, and to him, it was.

Even his trusty pitchfork had doubled in size. It now closely resembled Neptune's trident rather than a regular farming pitchfork. He slowly stood to his feet, upgraded from a Psycho

Hillbilly to a monstrous gigantic gladiator Psycho Hillbilly. He was fucking massive. Matthew could work out nonstop for the rest of his life and never come close to this size. It was a Christmas miracle, only not. He still had Matthew's face, but that was all. The rest of his body was near unrecognisable.

His bigger, thicker, head was able to produce an even more sinister grin when he looked at himself and felt greatly satisfied with the upgrades. He had the same look in his eyes as he had before the transformation. An evil playful look that enjoyed the chase as much as the torture. That look which would still laugh if he hurled another pig at one of the girls. While his body had seemingly quadrupled in size his personality had stayed intact. He was the same evil nasty asshole, only physically superior. The body had changed but the mind was the same. Perfect he thought.

The bolts of lightning were replaced by sheet lightning that enabled Abby and Whitney to see directly in front of them. The moon started to fight back bringing light to the farm once more, and with it a new sense of danger. It took their eyes a moment to adjust before they could clearly see Psycho Hillbilly standing there in all his transformed glory. It didn't take him long to stare back at them either. No sooner had they spotted him, he had turned and looked in their direction.

"Ok," Abby said looking at the enormous hulking figure in front of them.

"Time to go," she followed with while Whitney was still gulping at the sight of the newly upgraded Psycho Hillbilly. Part of her was paralysed with fear. In the back of her mind, she had thought this was over. She though she had killed Psycho Hillbilly, and Abby had decimated his mom. She thought all was left now was to get the fuck out of here and find a way home. But another part of her knew she was never leaving this farm. Whatever this nightmare was she was trapped in was never going to end. That thought was now a clear fact as she stood looking at the previously dead Psycho Hillbilly grinning back at her with his new monstrous look and even deadlier pitchfork. Whitney was once again going to be torn apart by this psycho fuck, maybe even worse than the other times.

Abby took a step forward but it was too late to run. A pile of hay running the length of the barn entrance inexplicably caught fire blocking off their only escape route while the shadow of Psycho Hillbilly behind the fire began to draw closer. They were trapped, and he was coming.

Stalking Upgrade

Abby looked at the fire in utter amazement. She couldn't see how it could possibly have started. No one had set it alight, there was no lightning strike that could have caused it, and no petrol had leaked from the truck. Even if there was a leak there wasn't anything to spark it. As far as Abby could surmise, the hay had just set itself on fire the second they tried to escape the barn. Abby looked upwards in disgust. She wasn't sure why she felt the urge to direct her rant upwards like she was giving them the power of gods or something, but if this was somehow the Splatploitation Brothers World then she knew they'd be looking down on her. Plus she'd shouted to the side all fucking evening and no one had answered her once.

"This is exactly the contrived bullshit I talk about in my reviews," Abby yelled. "Was that hay even there a few minutes ago? Even if it was, what the fuck set it on fire?" She added. Her face was a picture of fury, mixed with so many other things. At the forefront of those other things was the fact their only escape route had been impossibly blocked off. Close behind was the frustration of the whole evening's events taking their toll. Much like Whitney, Abby had hoped killing Hillbilly Mom after Whitney had rundown Psycho Hillbilly would somehow lead to the end of his dreadful evening. Like they'd broken the curse or something. Yet this fucking nightmare continued.

Almost equally annoying as the horrors of the night was the nature of the world they were stuck in. In Abby's head, she had decided if this was their world then they had control over it. They were writing the story so to speak, and from a creative standpoint, their writing was pathetic. How could they just change things on a whim that previously had no set up? How dare they just bring their villain back? Worst of all, how dare they block her fucking escape route without so much as a thought to how it happened? Would it have been so hard for the petrol from the truck to have leaked and then have the lightning ignite it? That would be impossible in its own right she thought. But within the context of wherever the fuck she was stuck that could happen. But no, they couldn't even be bothered to figure that out. Fucking hacks.

If Abby had thought about it harder she would have realised that this wasn't just a Splatploitation Brother thing. Plenty of horror films pulled these tricks, and the main slasher always returned. She'd be hard pressed to name a slasher film where the killer hadn't got up after absolute death. But she didn't care about any of that. Her anger was directed at the Splatploitation Brothers and everything shit that was happening was their fault as far as she was concerned.

"And don't you dare tell me it was the lightning," Abby added, just to keep on talking and possibly suggest they should have used that. Like a sneaky way to giving script notes. Abby continued her stare upwards waiting for answers while Whitney's gaze shifted from the fire to Abby as she wondered if her new friend was broken.

Abby's eyes briefly levelled on what stood in front as she watched the massive Psycho Hillbilly draw closer and closer while looking bigger and bigger with every step. This only enraged her further as she once again looked upwards hoping the Splatploitation Brothers were somehow listening.

"And in what part of the movie exactly did Psycho Hillbilly double in size and turn into a fucking Gladiator? Did I nod off for that bit? It's just plain lazy, you bunch of fucking incompetent assholes!"

Much like the level of violence committed this evening was much more than Abby had carried out the rest of her life combined, she was pretty certain she'd sworn more than ever too. But fuck it, these assholes deserved it is what she would have thought with a wry smile if she wasn't so pissed off.

"Who are you talking to?" Whitney finally asked through gritted teeth almost embarrassed for her new friend. Her attention had returned to the raging Psycho Hillbilly who hadn't stopped his march forward, but she was beginning to wonder if Abby had chosen this time to crack up. She got it, she wanted to just go crazy too. It almost felt like a comfort at this point. But she needed Abby clear-headed and thinking if they were going to get out of this latest mess.

"I'm talking to them bastard fuck-wit Splatploitation Brothers," Abby replied with pure anger in her voice, although the anger was directed at them, not Whitney. "If this is their world then I know they're somehow watching or listening. I also know they're there because of that piece of shit in front of us," Abby added with extra venom. "You were fucking roadkill you white trash inbred fuck," she shouted at the newly upgraded Psycho Hillbilly in one last attempt to let out all her rage and exhaust the remaining swear words she knew. The moment Abby called Psycho Hillbilly an inbred fuck the fire in front of them suddenly extinguished. Gone the way it came, out of the blue with no reason for its existence or demise.

With the fire out nothing stood between the ginormous Psycho Hillbilly and Abby and Whitney. Something did lay between them, however, as Psycho Hillbilly caught sight of his mom, or rather the mess that used to be her, lying dead on the ground. Abby followed the gaze of his cold eyes to the branding iron lying at her feet. Suddenly a lot of Abby's anger and rage towards the Splatploitation Brothers left her body as she became acutely aware of the more immediate threat right before her eyes. They could wait.

"Should we call it even?" She asked Psycho Hillbilly not expecting any kind of answer other than him ripping her apart.

Whitney for her part tried a smile to suggest that was a great idea, but Psycho Hillbilly had zero intention of calling a truce.

Abby snatched the trusty branding iron from the floor. She noticed for the first time that the branding iron had the letters HF shaped into it. The thick letters were surrounded by a metal circle giving the branding iron some sturdiness at the tip. It had been used plenty of times on animals and teens alike within the farm and never lost its shape. The most recent use of the branding iron had been the complete destruction of Hillbilly Mom. Some of her remains stuck to the lettering, and her blood still dripped from the circular part. Abby held the branding iron like a bat but was a lot less eager to charge Psycho Hillbilly with it than she had been his mum, no matter how successful the previous game plan had been.

Psycho Hillbilly dropped to his knees alongside his mutilated mother, however there wasn't a hint of emotion on his face. The girls expected there to be something with the gesture of kneeling beside her but he remained somewhat neutral, calm almost. It was as if he was taking in the mess and working out what to do with the information, but from a more clinical standpoint than the emotional one you'd expect from witnessing your mother beaten to a pulp. There was no remorse, no grief, nothing. Just coldness. In Abby's eyes it just made him all the more dangerous because she knew him destroying Whitney and herself was going to be his outlet. That was his way to grieve, not tears.

Abby considered for a brief moment taking the opportunity to bash his head in with the branding iron but up close he was even bigger than she first thought, and her first thought was that he was absolutely fucking massive. She wasn't even sure he would feel the connection, and that maybe it would feel like a fly landing on him. This wasn't a fight she could win, wasn't even one she felt she could start. She dropped the branding iron to the floor deciding if it wasn't going to help then it would probably only hinder in some way. Her eyes briefly caught sight of Hillbilly Mom's spiked rolling pin also sitting on the floor but she made no attempt for it. No, the right play here wasn't to fight in any way, shape, or form. It was to run like hell while he wasn't fully paying attention and the fire was extinguished.

Abby gestured Whitney towards the door while Psycho Hillbilly remained on his knees. But before she'd even finished taking her first step he stood, like he had sensed her movement. There was no getting around him.

Whitney looked at him not quite catching onto Abby's resignation of him being too big. Somehow they were going to have to battle this monster, she thought. Whitney didn't like their odds and had almost resigned herself to being killed once more, but she wasn't writing them off completely just yet. She'd faced death already tonight and survived. Maybe luck was still on their side. She didn't think they could kill him, but maybe knocking him off his feet in order to run by him would be enough. They'd beaten him before, not even that long ago in fact, but the person standing in front of them was barely recognisable from that asshole. He was an altogether different proposition. In fact, the only thing that hadn't changed about him was the first thing they would have both changed. That fucking accent.

"Time to get butchered," he said with his awful familiar drawl and in a one-liner fashion. If Abby had to guess she thought the line was probably meant to be a pun on them being in an abattoir, but it just didn't work with him holding a pitchfork instead of a butcher's knife. It shouldn't be the sort of thing she was thinking, but despite her predicament she still had how much of a bunch of hacks the Splatploitation Brothers were on her mind. She knew she needed to drop such thoughts for the moment because not for the first time tonight she was facing a life or death situation. Abby couldn't help herself. It was just the way her mind worked.

Psycho Hillbilly's sadistic grim spread across his face once more. The one look he had Abby further critiqued before realising once again it wouldn't help their situation. He had nothing but evil intentions and they had no way of really getting past him despite Whitney's best hopes. That's what Abby needed to be concentrating on. He lunged forward after climbing from his knees and swung the massive pitchfork. Abby jumped to the right; Whitney fell to the left. With one swing he had already separated them and made his job easier. No longer were they thinking about how to get around him, now they were on the run.

Both had sprinted towards the entanglement of machinery. Abby looked back for Whitney only now realising they'd gone separate ways.

"Why would you split up?" she muttered to herself as she saw Whitney going in the opposite direction. For the moment however, Whitney was safe. Psycho Hillbilly had spent all day torturing and chasing the poor girl, now he had fresh meat in the form of Abby to play with.

"You're going to regret hitting me from behind, you sneaky bitch," he told Abby with far too much joy in his voice and sounding exactly the same despite the transformation. For someone who had just become roadkill and seen his mom as paste on the deck, he was certainly in a chipper mood. He ran his pitchfork against the metal of a nearby machine. The scrapes and clangs formed an awful metal sound that cut right through Abby's ears but seemed to perfectly fit the situation as sparks flew from the point of the pitchfork.

He wanted her to try and run. Was practically begging her to in his own nasty way. He liked the feeling of the chase and had a renewed need for it. The urge to finish them off quickly that had taken hold in the boneyard had subsided to the need to create more fear. The need to make them feel helpless. He loved that feeling, it was one of his biggest thrills.

As much as Abby didn't want to oblige she didn't really have a choice as he stepped forward nearing a distance where he could take her head off with one powerful swing of his mammoth pitchfork. Abby took a big step back as she tried to create more distance between them but stopped when she felt the heel of her foot against the beginnings of the metal chute leading into the Slaughterhouse behind her.

Despite being backed into a corner Abby absolutely and positively refused to run into that mess of buzzing saws, moving platforms, and hooks which contained the remnants of dead people. It was ridiculous. It was stupid how this barn was the way it was in the first place. No fucking way should it be a Slaughterhouse. No way should half of the machines in said Slaughterhouse even be here. They made absolutely no sense and she knew they were only there purely for effect, for the visual aesthetic. But especially she knew no way should she be running into all of that, not a chance. That's just something a dumb horror character would do that no real person would ever even dream of.

But... Abby couldn't think of any other option as Psycho Hillbilly viciously swung his pitchfork and nearly took her face clean off. Abby took another step back from the force off the swing before she turned and ran up the funnelled chute much to the delight of Psycho Hillbilly. His revenge was going to be brutal and he could hardly wait so he too took a step on to the chute readying to slaughter Abby.

*

Watching the madness unfold in the comfort of their private

cinema back at the bottom of the Splatploitation Brothers Studio was the gang themselves. The mood in the room had drastically changed with smiles and popcorn and drinks. Oh my! The whole cinematic experience at its finest.

On the screen in front of them, they watched as Abby entered the barbaric chute and Psycho Hillbilly followed. The screen showed a close-up of Abby's worried face as apparently, this magical setup edited itself, and the Splatploitation Brothers all cheered at the sight. Roger threw some popcorn connecting with Abby's nose on the screen and the group cheered once more. Percy's smile grew.

"Now this is more my vision," he proudly announced.

Funhouse

Abby spotted a track running directly above her head as she ascended the moving travelator within the chute. Hanging from the track was a bunch of evenly spaced grim metal hooks that all had discoloured chunks of meat and dried blood stuck to them. The hooks looked like they'd love to add Abby to their killing history as they glided menacingly above her.

Behind her she heard the heavy footsteps of the monstrous Psycho Hillbilly. The hooks hung alongside him, close to head height in his massive new form, but he didn't care. He just brushed them aside, barely acknowledging their existence. He had tunnel vision for Abby. She had regretted entering the chute the moment she stumbled onto it, but now with Psycho Hillbilly chasing her the danger had increased tenfold.

As if to emphasise the danger a bolt gun took aim and fired at Abby from her left side. The bolt barely missed Abby and crashed hard against the other side of the narrow chute denting the metalwork. Such was the force a direct hit would have killed her. A fate many cows and teens had suffered before her. She spotted a second bolt gun coming in line with her as the floor continued to move beneath Abby's feet. While the floor wasn't moving quickly it was still hard to go against it, like swimming upstream, so Abby couldn't turn back and just had to face whatever lay ahead. Plus with Psycho Hillbilly directly behind her turning back wasn't really an option anyway.

Abby rolled out of the way of the second shot as the clang of metal on metal once again echoed throughout the Slaughterhouse above the loud noises already escaping the machines. If she couldn't go back then she'd just have to awesomely tackle this ridiculous setup by ducking and rolling, she thought in a pretty childish way. The successful roll had avoided the shot much to Abby's delight but it had also taken Abby out of the thin chute and onto a new long and winding conveyor belt. She was no longer the cattle being killed per se, which was a relief, but was part of the cattle being processed instead.

Before Abby could get her bearings a different type of hook snatched her leg. This one wasn't setting her up in a position to be shot and killed by a bolt, this one was setting her up to be ground up or made into cuts. Abby was pulled upwards and left hanging upside down, suspended in the air with her skimpy top hanging down towards her face. She hadn't thought about the awful outfit in a while, but although in the most danger she had been in all night, she was hating the fact that her tummy was on full display. Especially now knowing the Splatploitation Brothers were probably watching.

The hook had dug itself into Abby's left shoe. If she was in better shape she would have been able to lean upwards and undo the shoe to escape, but flexibility wasn't one of Abby's strengths. And honestly how many people could actually do that anyway? Instead she just helplessly hung there as she heard Psycho Hillbilly step on to the same conveyor belt.

"Is my kebab ready yet?" he chuckled as he caught sight of Abby hanging feebly from the hook. His laughter was enough to make her feel sick, even more so than the smell of meat and blood that had followed her throughout the Slaughterhouse.

The place really did fucking stink. She thought there was a bit of a whiff in the air when they first entered the barn but put it down to the rotten-looking hay, mostly because she hadn't seen the Slaughterhouse behind her. Abby still wasn't convinced the Slaughterhouse was there to begin with but that debate would have to wait for another time. The smell she first smelt however was nothing compared to this. This place smelt worse than the pit she started in, worse than the swamp, the pigpen, worse than anything she'd ever smelt before in her entire life. This was fucking foul. Even from her upside-down position it was easy to see why. There was just blood and rank meat everywhere. Every hook was covered, every metal sheet on the various platforms sprayed, every machine had blood splattered against it. It all looked purposeful too. Abby was sure an abattoir produced a lot of blood and shit, but this seemed far too much even for that. This seemed like decoration or set dressing, which it could have easily been.

Psycho Hillbilly slowly made his way towards Abby but his enormous mass was unsteady on the moving platform. He had to use the giant pitchfork to keep his balance like some kind of hideous tightrope walker. Every step he took teetered him towards the edge of the belt and whatever waited below. He wanted to catch up with her sooner. Wanted to take a bite out of that exposed stomach, maybe even punch her in the face as she had him. He just wanted to have a good laugh while fucking her up, but he couldn't get close to her at the moment. Just had to enjoy Abby being helpless until he caught up.

Abby watched as he licked his lips and started to dribble at the thought of how best to destroy her. He was positively glowing despite his very visible struggle at navigating the conveyor belt. She could see his eyes narrow in on her stomach and she wanted it to all end at that moment. But what an awful last moment that would be. Some massive disgusting-looking Psycho Hillbilly perving over her while she hung upside down in a Slaughterhouse. That couldn't be it. Her thoughts once again drifted to how ridiculous this all was. She fucking hated every second of this world. Yeah, she'd given the Splatploitation Brothers a bad review but the punishment most definitely did not fit the crime in her eyes and she'd make sure they knew that if she ever got the chance. Fucking assholes.

The hook swung Abby away from looking at Psycho

Hillbilly to show her what was in store ahead. At first, she was relieved not to be looking at that piece of shit but her foul mood got worse when she spotted what was waiting. At the end of the long conveyor belt was a metal sheet with different cuts of meat stencilled onto it. Multiple spinning saws spun rapidly on the outline of each design ready to make the desired cut of meat.

"That's not how animal cuts are made, you fucking losers!" Abby screamed at the top of her lungs seeing the buzzing saws and stencilled outlines ahead. It didn't matter anymore that she couldn't reach her feet to untie herself, she had to try. She had to do something. Abby swung herself upwards but gained little height. She tried again with her arms stretched out as far as they could go but didn't come close. She tried with all her might to sit herself up and reach her trainers but she just didn't have the strength to do it. She had never in her life had the strength to lift her whole body up like that despite the climbing, but that hadn't ever been a problem before. Now it meant life or death.

She gave up stretching and tried to wiggle herself free instead. Why the hell did her shoes fit so well? Why couldn't they have been a little big on her? She just needed something to go her way. Abby could hear the spinning saws ahead of her now above any other sound in the noisy abattoir. They spun with delight as their latest prey drew closer. She was certain they had sped up from the first time she looked at them. They were so desperate to cut her into ribs and loins and shanks and whatever else was written on that ridiculous nonsensical stencil they had sped up to slice her a millisecond quicker. Obviously. that's not really how saws work, the distance would be the same no matter the speed, but Abby was pissed off and wanted to be angry at everything no matter how unreasonable some of her thoughts and logic had become.

I mean seriously, what the fuck was that stencil, it was stupid. Was she in a cartoon now because she was certain this was the sort of thing that could only exist in a *Looney Tunes* sketch. Not in the real world, or whatever version of the real world this place was. How hard would it have been for them to do a little research and see how the different cuts were achieved, just Google that shit. But no. Instead they design some weird metal sheet with all the cuts drawn out like fucking toddlers. She really did hate them. That pepper spray in Roger's face and kick to Matthew's balls felt too little now. She had let them off lightly. Especially if they were going to slice her up into a bunch of different meat cuts over nothing.

Psycho Hillbilly knocked another hook aside as he took a successful giant step forward. He was getting the hang of the conveyor belt finally and had gained some ground on Abby. He was almost within arm's reach of her and beaming at her current state. He looked towards the metal sheet with joy seeing Abby had no chance of escaping. "Going to make nuggets out of you," he bellowed. Sure enough, nuggets were stencilled onto the metal sheet with the accompanying saws.

Abby gave up the fight. She couldn't even be bothered to tell him how moronic his comment was. Didn't have the spirit left in her to verbally put him down one last time. She couldn't reach upwards and hadn't been able to successfully swing sidewards. She couldn't wiggle out of the trainers and the odds of her just falling free from the shoe breaking didn't seem very likely. She cursed herself for running up that chute, she knew she shouldn't have. Had told herself not to. That's the kind of stupid shit they do in horrors only to get themselves killed. She had reasoned there was no other option, but that hadn't helped her. In hindsight, she'd reacted the complete opposite way to which she always told herself she would. She'd failed the scream queen horror challenge. All that time spent mocking dumb movie characters and the first chance she got she did exactly the same fucking thing.

She thought about Psycho Hillbilly kneeling beside his dead mother and how she should have taken the chance to attack him then. She knew she would fail, she had that feeling, but it had to be better than this. It had to be better than hanging upside down with her stomach on display ready to be cut into pieces while Psycho Hillbilly laughed in her face. She should have risked attacking him.

Now it was over. He was right, she was about to be made into chicken nuggets and the only thought that gave her any comfort was maybe this idiot would be dragged into the spinning saws as well because he seemed blissfully unaware that he was on the same course. But then she remembered he wasn't attached to any hook. He'd probably just hop off after she became a steak. Her last half-smile of being avenged straight away faded. What a fucking lousy way to go.

Whitney Saves Abby

Abby may have accepted her fate but Whitney wasn't ready to see her brand new friend die anytime soon. She especially wasn't ready to see her diced up into meat cuts after the way her previous friends had ended up as smudges on the pavement. She had run in the opposite direction to Abby when the initial attack happened but had circled around when she had realised it was Abby being chased by Psycho Hillbilly, not her. Whitney had watched Abby on the top conveyor belt and seen the hook snatch her leg and begin to lead her towards that crazy spinning saw metal sheet thingy. She then watched as Psycho Hillbilly slowly gained ground on Abby and knew without her intervention Abby was done for. She couldn't allow that to happen.

Whitney made her way towards the platform and began to climb the blindside of the machine. It wasn't a hard climb, but she was exhausted. The day had taken its toll ten times over so the relatively simple climb did have its challenges. One such challenge was getting on to the long travelator itself. The travelator track didn't have any sides, the track just run directly over a metal pathway, so after climbing the machine Whitney had to then drag herself on to the track while it was moving. A tough ask at the best of times, let alone when Whitney was tired, sore, and just wanted to go to bed. For a moment Whitney didn't think she was going to make it in time as Abby drew nearer the machine and Psycho Hillbilly closed in, but Whitney pushed herself hard to get on to the track. This was something she had to do, she had to save Abby.

Abby helplessly watched as the spinning saws got ready to eat her up. She cringed at the cocktail of sounds consisting of the anticipating saws and Psycho Hillbilly's disgusting laugh that lingered in the air. It sucked that not only was she going to die, but she was going to die entertaining that motherfucker. Then someone grabbed her foot. She hadn't expected it so it took Abby a moment to figure out what was happening. She thought at first that maybe Psycho Hillbilly had decided on one last torture, maybe he wanted to do the killing himself, but the idea didn't match the lightness of the grab. It was too delicate for it to be that oaf. Abby managed to spin herself slightly and see Whitney on the travelator alongside her.

Whitney desperately tried to yank Abby's foot free from the hook. She couldn't lift Abby out of the shoe, and couldn't tear the shoe off the hook, so she did the only practical thing left and untied Abby's shoelaces to slide her foot free. Abby slammed onto the conveyor-belt track with her shoe nearly hitting her on the way down as now it decided to finally break. Psycho Hillbilly caught sight of Whitney but it was too late to prevent the rescue. It didn't mean he couldn't retaliate though.

He thrust his pitchfork forward towards Whitney who was left standing there with an almost guilty look on her face. As if she'd been caught with her hand in the cookie jar rather than saving her friend from a horrific death by saws. The massive pitchfork pierced Whitney's side just as she finished freeing her friend. Abby screamed as Whitney fell from the travelator while holding the pitchfork that had partially skewed her. Abby hadn't seen how much damage the pitchfork had done but knew the giant weapon wouldn't have taken Whitney lightly as Whitney disappeared over the side.

Abby couldn't do anything to help Whitney as the spinning saws were about to take their chance and slice Abby to pieces. Whitney would have to wait, and so would everything else as the only thing Abby could do to avoid certain death was to get off the travelator herself. She tumbled off the opposite side to Whitney and landed awkwardly on a new moving platform which was just a different dangerous place to the safe place she'd hoped for. Her ankle twisted on impact but for the moment she was at least away from Psycho Hillbilly who now suddenly realised he was next in line for the nugget maker.

He tried to get off the platform but couldn't move his feet in time. Couldn't get them sorted to either make the jump off the platform or lower himself down to the one Abby was on. Instead, he came head to head with the metal sheet and spinning saws that had just been cheated out of tearing Abby apart. They seemed happy enough with the alternative option of the much larger Psycho Hillbilly.

Psycho Hillbilly planted his hands against the metal sheet in the only spaces available away from the saws. He kept his arms straight and his face back but the battle wasn't just a test of upper body strength. Push as he might against the metal sheet and saws, it didn't help the lower half of his body. The platform was still moving and pulled his feet towards the deadly metal sheet. He kept his legs moving in the opposite direction for the moment, but that was only a short-term solution as he was already beginning to tire.

His feet kept sliding towards the spinning saws on the bottom half of the metal cutmaker and he couldn't work out any way to stop it from happening. It wasn't possible to put his feet against the side of the conveyor belt because it didn't have one as such. It wasn't built like an escalator at a shopping mall, it didn't need sides as in theory almost everything was meant to be hanging on hooks. The travelator was largely there just to collect the mess and spillage. The very thing that had made it difficult for Whitney to rescue Abby in the first place was now making it equally difficult for Psycho Hillbilly to escape. It appeared the Slaughterhouse had no real bias and just wanted to slice up everyone.

One of the saws took a swipe at Psycho Hillbilly's ankle

while he was contemplating what to do next. It cut through his overalls but didn't quite reach his skin. He tried pulling his legs back but that only unbalanced his top half. His face was a whisker away from the loin template which even he would have reasoned didn't make any sense.

He pushed harder trying his best to get away from the machine but the travelator continued to bring him closer to the saws. Just moments ago he was excitedly waiting for the spinning saws to cut Abby into juicy pieces and now here he was desperately trying to prevent that from happening to him. Worse still, she didn't get diced up in the slightest. He wasn't a fan of irony, and he wasn't a fan of this travelator either. Any time he pushed his top half away from the saws his bottom half got into more danger. Then anytime he readjusted for that he found himself face to face with the saws again. Or rather nose to nose as one of the saws sliced the tip of his nose straight off.

It happened in an instant. He was so busy trying to get his feet out of the way of the lower saws that he lost his balance. His hands momentarily crumbled with too much weight on them and that was enough for his body to jerk forward. He tried to move his head back in time but wasn't quick enough. The loin cutter had its chance and took it, slicing the tip of Psycho Hillbilly's nose clean off. Blood fountained from his nose spraying the metal sheet and anything else in the immediate area while the tip of his nose sailed through the air never to be seen again.

It wasn't the whole juicy cut the machine was designed for but finally, it had tasted flesh this evening and now wanted more. Psycho Hillbilly pushed back with all his might now fully understanding the seriousness of his predicament. He was desperate to cover his nose and stop some of the bleeding but no way was he moving either hand after regaining some sort of balance. He just had to watch as more blood cascaded from his nose on to the moving pathway below. What a fucking horrible few minutes, he thought as the pain from his nose, or now lack of, fully kicked in.

Abby had watched the machine take a slice of Psycho Hillbilly's nose but couldn't celebrate as she was dealing with a new machine of her own. Metres in front of Abby was the giant metal stamper currently turning a small pile of bones into powder and would soon be doing the same to Abby if she didn't act right away.

"What the hell is that even for?" She shouted out in disgust.

Bone fragments sprayed from the machine as the loud stamps became deafening with each new slam.

Abby's ankle hurt from the fall from the previous moving walkway but luckily she only had to swivel herself round to hop off this belt. This time there was no hook restraining her so she managed to escape the possibility of being turned into dust with relative ease, albeit still a little too close for comfort. She'd got off the machine to the side that took her even further away from Whitney as she collapsed to the Slaughterhouse floor. For the moment she was happy to be on solid ground again, even if it was a filthy disgusting nasty disease-ridden Slaughterhouse floor.

She looked upwards in time to see the spinning saws take a second chunk of Psycho Hillbilly. This one took a slice off his knees. Psycho Hillbilly buckled, dropped to the very knees that had just been cut open which caused a second round of pain to scream from them. The task of keeping away from the metal sheet had become infinitely more difficult now that he couldn't keep stepping back, while his knees felt like they were on fire. Blood poured from the new wound and dripped off the sides of the travelator mixing with the previous nose blood. If the machine didn't finishing him off the bleeding out might. Psycho Hillbilly now had to push his entire body away from the machine, not just his upper half, and it was a battle he couldn't win.

He turned away from the saws trying to stop them taking the rest of his nose but they settled for his cheek instead. Sliced it open like one of those cheese cutters where you lower the wire down. Once again blood sprayed from the cut covering any part of the metal sheets that wasn't already blood-soaked. The saws ate the blood up and flung it further into the Slaughterhouse as they spun. The whole scene looked absolutely grotesque with the metal sheet now painted red and the travelator sliding along covered in Psycho Hillbilly's blood. The floors and roofs hadn't been spared either. Every part of the Slaughterhouse seemed drenched with an increasing amount of the blood coming fresh from Psycho Hillbilly. Abby had no sympathy for the cunt. He was getting what he deserved. She just hoped it stuck this time and he ended up dead dead with no do-overs.

Abby tried to stand wanting to see the blades make their final blow and finish that monster off but her ankle was hurting too much. She had to settle for watching from the floor instead but didn't get the show she wanted anyway.

Psycho Hillbilly's muscles began to bulge as he forced himself back to his feet momentarily ignoring the pain in his diced knees and being careful where he put his hands. The push upwards resulted in him falling forward somewhat leaving him mere millimetres away from his whole body being sucked into the deadly saws. He had no choice, all or nothing. He flung himself backwards from the metal sheet hoping he'd fall over the side before he was dragged into the saws. Mercifully for Psycho Hillbilly he disappeared over the same side as Whitney before the travelator could take advantage and finish him off. A gutsy and fortunate escape.

Abby was disappointment at not seeing Psycho Hillbilly turned to mincemeat. In any normal situation the idea of being disappointed at not seeing someone get diced into meat cuts would haunt her, but this wasn't a normal situation. His being alive meant they were still in serious trouble, no matter how bad his fall looked. She knew by this point he could take it and would be stalking her again in no time.

Abby hauled herself towards a collection of metal troughs to her side. They were filled to the brim with blood. More hooks hung above them with plenty of leftover meat still clinging on. The floor itself was stained deeply red. This whole area was a total gore fest, gore galore, and Abby fitted in perfectly while still covered in parts of Psycho Hillbilly's Mum and some of his more recent blood too.

Standing beside the trough was a large machine with several vertical spinning saws. Abby hadn't noticed it when she landed but now used it to heave herself off the floor as she didn't trust the troughs. She didn't particularly trust this instrument of death either as the vertical saws munched together like they were waiting to eat her, but she had to get to her feet and find Whitney.

Whitney vs Upgrade

Whitney lay barely conscious on the Slaughterhouse floor surrounded by discarded flesh, dried blood, and some fresh new blood that the platform had recently thrown out after taking it from Psycho Hillbilly's nose and knees. The travelator continued to move above Whitney but she hadn't been able to focus on what happened since falling from it. Her eyesight felt blurry and the back of her head ached a lot. She didn't realise she had banged her head pretty hard on impact and could well have been concussed... again.

The pitchfork had freed itself from Whitney's grasp as she hit the floor and currently lay beside her. The initial strike had hardly caught her despite Psycho Hillbilly's best efforts. He was off-balance as he lunged forward and lost his grip of the weapon before impact. It had ripped into her side but not struck any major organ. More a glancing blow than an impale. She'd taken a few shots to her side already this evening and one more wouldn't kill her, but she was somewhat riding her luck as kill her it would have if it had been an inch to the side.

Whitney clutched the back of her head as the building pain finally reached her. She pulled her blood-soaked hand away from the back of her head confused whether it was her own blood or some left over from the filthy floor. Unfortunately for Whitney the blood was too wet and warm for it to have been left over from whatever massacre last took place here. Before she could fully comprehend what that meant she caught a glimpse of movement.

Beginning to try and stand a few metres away from her was the torn up bloody Psycho Hillbilly. He was missing half his nose, and one side of his face looked like it had been ripped clean off, but he still had the same sadistic smile as he spotted

Whitney lying defenceless on the floor beside him.

"Why, fancy seeing you here," he mustered trying to fight the pain from his knees that had been completely shredded. He looked a complete mess, but that had never stopped him before and certainly wasn't going to stop him now. He gazed at the hapless vulnerable young lady once again ready to make this the worst night of her life.

Whitney forgot her own pain for the moment and tried to crawl away from him. She didn't get too far however as her crawls were slow and ineffective, she could barely push herself forward let alone make up any kind of ground. Her eyes were still blurry and she felt like she could doze off at any moment. Her whole body was weak and mostly unresponsive. She'd been lying in a puddle of her own blood and was only just realising her head was possibly cracked open. Blood dripped from her hair leaving a trail that marked her lack of progress. The idea of moving just seemed an impossibility to Whitney at this point but as always she tried. Slow snail-paced progress was still progress.

Psycho Hillbilly was far less groggy despite being carved up and taking the same fall. The old him probably wouldn't have survived any of that, and Whitney wouldn't have needed to try and crawl away. But the new him, with this massive new body and muscles he didn't even know could exist, not only had he survived it, he'd relished it. It was a far greater test of his new physical attributes than these annoying little girls could ever be. Despite missing half his nose and his face being somewhat ripped apart, and despite his knees looking and feeling like shit, he felt invincible. Scratch that, he was invincible, he grinned.

He grabbed his prone pitchfork from the floor and used it as a crutch to help himself get the rest of the way up. His knees buckled once or twice and a little more of his cheek fell off but eventually, he got to his feet. OK maybe he wasn't quite invincible, but still, everything considered he was in remarkable shape. His smile widened as he saw Whitney's pathetic attempt to get away from him. She'd barely made it a few metres let alone out of sight.

"Will you still do anything for me?" he asked enjoying the moment. Sure it had been a shit last few minutes all things considered, but all of that was already starting to leave his mind. He had survived and was now enjoying himself once more. The chase was again on, albeit one that felt like it was in slow motion.

Whitney continued her painstakingly laboured crawl. Ahead of her stood a single heavy door with a small circled window near the top. She had no clue what was on the other side of the door but focused on having to reach it. Gave herself a goal. She had to distract herself from her throbbing head and bloody side, and that fucking deranged lunatic baiting her from behind.

"We could have a nice evening in together," Psycho Hillbilly suggested without an ounce of earnest in his voice as he answered the question for her. He couldn't even keep a straight face as he said it. He grabbed a left over chunk of raw meat from a nearby hook and took a bite.

"Could have a nice meal together," he suggested with his mouth full before spitting the chewed up raw meat over Whitney. He laughed as it tangled with her blood-soaked hair.

Whitney hadn't noticed the disgusting act. Her eyes were still facing forward away from him and focused on the door in front of her. She had heard his taunts all night, whatever he had to say was nothing new to her. That didn't stop him talking though as he continued to enjoy his dominance. He'd pushed the pain from his knees to one side and was walking properly without the need of the pitchfork to assist him. This meant he could use it as a weapon again.

"With some fresh meat," he bellowed in response to his own

previous statement and slammed the enormous pitchfork down. It landed inches away from Whitney's foot but she didn't so much as blink. Didn't even realise what had happened. She was feeling so, so tired, every part of her ached, she could barely see anything and felt the colour draining out of her body. All she wanted to do was get to the other side of that door and sleep. Nothing else mattered, including Psycho Hillbilly trying to scare her with his oversized pitchfork.

"And then you can get back to licking my pitchfork," Psycho Hillbilly howled as if he'd been storing that punchline up all night, which he had. His vile obnoxious laugh filled the barn but was quickly interrupted.

"Where are you hiding you dumb fucking hick!" Abby shouted. She sounded close to Psycho Hillbilly but he couldn't work out what direction the taunt had come from. He stopped laughing in an attempt to try and work out where she was momentarily forgetting about the dying girl on the floor.

"I think I just stepped in your mom," Abby added with more than a tinge of nastiness in her voice. With Psycho Hillbilly distracted Whitney made up more ground getting to the door. She could recognise Abby's voice in the haze she was in but hadn't really been able to do anything with that. She felt relieved Abby was still alive but couldn't shout out or help her or do anything. The only thing that mattered was the door. Whitney finally reached the metal door after using the motivation of Abby still being alive to push her pace a little harder for the last few crawls.

Whitney grabbed upwards and found the handle to the door. She had to stand slightly to swing the door open and managed to do just that, albeit using the last of her reserves. She crashed landed inside the meat locker with her eyes barely open and her head spinning. Carcasses of both people and animals hung from the low ceiling and broken crates were piled in every corner. Ice peels from the walls had reformed into awkward shapes and given the room a more ice cave feel to it than that of a normal storage room. Layers of frost covered the floor Whitney was spread across with the temperature in the room easily below freezing. The room couldn't have looked any colder. Just like a big block of ice had been hollowed out.

From behind her Whitney heard the door shut and lock. She spun round and looked upwards to the small circled window to see Psycho Hillbilly looking down on her from the other side. He held up five fingers and mouthed to her, 'back in five,' before disappearing out of sight. Whitney didn't care if he was coming back or not. Her thoughts were no longer clear enough to think.

She lay on the floor with the icy coldness numbing the pains in her body and the back of her head. Her bloody wet hair had already begun to stick to the floor but that was far from her mind. Her eyes finally closed and her mind drifted to nowhere. She wasn't sure if she'd ever open her eyes again as she allowed the coldness to take her. She'd battled hard, done everything she could. She'd survived longer than she ever had before, and had saved her new friend from certain death, but Whitney's fight was over. It was up to Abby now.

Abby vs Upgrade

Psycho Hillbilly scraped his pitchfork along the ground as he navigated the noisy machinery in search of Abby. He always liked doing that while hunting down his victims, it put the fear of God into them, he thought. Made them shit their pants. Whether it did or not he never got round to asking, but in his mind, it was a total power move. Twisted wires hung from half the machines, sparks fell from others, however, it was all for show. None of these machines had any real purpose in a Slaughterhouse and a Slaughterhouse had no purpose being in a barn. The whole place made no sense but that hadn't stopped it from claiming many lives and Psycho Hillbilly wanted to add two more to his list.

"I'm going to eat you raw for what you did to my mom, little girl," Psycho Hillbilly coarsely shouted. He listened for Abby's response still trying to decide in what direction she was. He had worked his way around half the barn but this place really was a maze. It had way too many machines in which half of them linked together creating a long path and the other half created dead ends. There were also plenty of huge pipes and thick wires tangled together blocking off more paths as well as creating new ones. It wasn't an economical streamlined approach, more a toss everything together to see what happens approach.

He wasn't even sure if he could work his way back to Whitney, but she wasn't going anywhere. He didn't have to worry about that. Could finish her off later if she wasn't already dead. For the moment he wanted the other one. He knew the barn only had one exit and he was sure Abby wouldn't leave without her friend. That sort of loyalty was what was going to get her killed. She should have run when she had the chance rather than baiting him, now he was going to slowly tear her apart and she only had herself to blame.

Psycho Hillbilly had killed quite a few teens in this place over the years. As much as he loved to torture and kill them in the farmhouse, or the immediate surroundings like he had Whitney's slutty friends, often he'd make his way here for some extra fun. He reckoned he'd killed a teen using every machine in this place at least once over his many years of terror. Hell, even his mom had shot the odd whore with the bolt gun. She didn't like to tease them the way he did, or at least she hadn't when she was alive, he nostalgically thought for a brief moment before getting his game face back on.

He looked up at the metal stencil cut sheet with its saws still buzzing at the end of the travelator. That had been his favourite machine over the years but he looked at it less favourably today. His hand instinctively went to his nose but he pulled it back without touching it. It still stung. He had circled the barn and reached the other side where Abby had fallen, but she wasn't there. She must be close, he thought while looking up at the sheet again with a desire to rip it off its hinges and fucking destroy it for what it had done to him today. But then he remembered the joy it would have brought if it had sliced Abby into pieces, and all the fun times they'd had together in the past. A scorpion has to sting he would have further thought if he considered things in those terms. Instead, it just had his respect for the pain and destruction it had caused.

Psycho Hillbilly turned and reached the enormous metal stamping machine. He caught sight of some bloody footprints on the other side of the stamper leading in a new direction. The footprints were too small to be his own and Whitney couldn't walk, so they had to be Abby's. He began to climb over the machine to follow the footprints he hoped would lead to that troublesome little bitch Abby when a jolt of electricity surged through his body. But this electricity wasn't like the sort that had restarted his black heart and upgraded his body. This electricity was only designed to induce pain.

Abby stood behind Psycho Hillbilly tightly gripping a cattle prod that she continued to hold against him. She jabbed it deep into his stomach and wasn't going to let go. The electricity raced through Psycho Hillbilly as he collapsed onto the conveyor belt leading towards the pointless, but destructive, metal stamp machine. He landed heavily on the belt with his body sprawled across it. His legs hung off the side but the travelator didn't care about that as it proceeded to drag him closer to the giant stamp.

He was still writhing and squirming from the electricity running through his veins when he looked up in time to see the belt had carried him all the way underneath the giant stamp. He had no time to do anything about it, just look up and see the unforgiving giant thick metal square hurtling down towards him.

CRUNCH.

The metal squished Psycho Hillbilly without any further thought. It may not serve any real purpose within the abattoir but the one job it did have for whatever reason, it did extremely well. Abby dropped the cattle prod at the sound of the crunch. Barely able to stand on her swollen ankle which was now back in its shoe, albeit it a rather ripped up and falling apart shoe, it was her turn for the one-liner.

"Should never fuck with a scream queen," she said with a grin further punctuating the menace in her voice. She enjoyed that despite the corniness of it all.

Abby turned away from the mess at the metal stamp to search for Whitney. She had a rough idea where Whitney landed but didn't know whether she was still alive. She had previously heard Psycho Hillbilly talking and hoped it was to Whitney, but whether Whitney was still alive at that point was uncertain. It wasn't beneath that asshole to taunt a dead body. From Abby's point of view the pitchfork had skewed Whitney in half, so for all she knew, Whitney was dead. Tears trickled down her face at the thought but she brushed them away. Alive until proven otherwise she decided. She took a step in Whitney's direction before stopping dead. Something stirred inside her, a gut feeling born out of the knowledge of binge-watching thousands of horror films.

"There's always a second scare," she told herself.

Abby slowly turned to see Psycho Hillbilly towering directly behind her showing his true height since the upgrade. His face had been completely squashed. What was left of his nose was turned upright giving him more of a snout look. One eye was swollen shut and possibly missing while the other was fractured and bloodshot. His mouth was broken with his teeth gone and lips split wide open. His jaw was hanging loose hiding whatever was left of his chin.

His exposed arms were missing any sense of skin and bones in the way they were before. It seemed impossible he could even use them. His bones were broken and pointing out in all directions. His skin had been ripped from the top half of his body when the unforgiving machine rose back up after squashing him. He looked like one of those anatomy models found in a science class.

The only things that stayed intact were his legs. They were still hanging from the belt when the heavy metal stamp came down. He'd been squished from the waist up leaving just the bottom half of his body to survive. But even then his knees were still a state from the saws. They looked ripped and shredded, albeit still an improvement from the top half of his body. There was just no fucking way he should be alive, let alone standing, let alone still fucking going after Abby. It was impossible and she knew it. He wasn't going to live for long, he was done, but as a slasher killer in a Splatploitation Brothers flick he had one more purpose. One more thing to do before he could die. He had to kill the scream queen which Abby had proclaimed herself as being moments earlier. Abby had seen enough slasher films to know better, and now she was going to pay the price for that gloating.

He grabbed Abby by the throat and thrust her towards the bloody troughs. She banged her head hard against the closest one and withered to the floor. Abby regained her bearings but not quickly enough as Psycho Hillbilly loomed over her once more leaving her nowhere to go. Viciously grabbing the back of her head he plunged her into the bath of blood awaiting inside the trough.

He tightly held her under the bloody water as she lashed out with any part of her body she could move. She knew he was weak, on death's door, but she couldn't make a good connection as her screams were lost in the blood. Abby gave up trying to hit him and instead grabbed the side of the trough trying to heave herself free as she gulped down more bloody water.

But he was a lot stronger than she was, even in his brutalised state. His arms shouldn't even be working with the way the bones were sticking out, but he still overpowered her. He pushed down harder giving Abby no chance at all as she went back to digging her fingers into the exposed muscle on his arms. He no longer had the normal sinister smile on his face, or offered his normal one-liners that he loved to dish out while killing because quite frankly he didn't have a face or mouth to express any of that. But inside what remained of his head he was enjoying this one last moment of triumph. This one last kill. Who knew if he'd be brought back again. Better to enjoy this moment he thought, as it could be his last. It was definitely going to be hers his grin would have suggested, could he have grinned.

Abby's fight began to fade. The last of her resistances escaped her body along with the last of her breaths. Bloody water was filling her lungs as Psycho Hillbilly didn't let up. He wasn't going to make the same mistake she did. He was seeing this through to the end and making sure the bitch was dead. He might not get to eat her as he had planned, but he was still going to fucking kill her and this did seem like a particularly nasty way for her to die.

He continued holding her beneath the water. Continued the bloody drowning as Abby's body went limp. He was set to kill her and exact his revenge. What a fucking crazy evening it had been. This wouldn't bring his mum back, it wouldn't bring him back either as he felt his life slowly draining, but it would lead to him dying with a smile. A smile on the inside only due to the lack of a mouth or lips.

His happy ending wasn't to be. Psycho Hillbilly was barged from behind and disappeared into the vertical saw machine which was beside the trough before he'd even fully acknowledged his happy inside smile. A spray of blood hit the barn roof as the saws chewed Psycho Hillbilly up until nothing was left. They didn't even take their time slowly drawing him in and chopping him up, it was as if they ate him whole. They weren't taking any chances of being robbed of a kill either.

Swamp Boy Saves The Day

Everything changed for Swamp Boy when that wooden plank connected with his head. Abby had swung hard and the plank had nails sticking from it. The bent nail wasn't an issue, that one just hurt. But the second nail, the one still standing straight in its original shape, that more than hurt. That killed.

Swamp Boy had felt the nail sink into his brain and for a moment he was dead, only he wasn't. He couldn't describe the feeling accurately but it was along the lines of the creature was dead, not him. Abby had somehow penetrated the monster's brain with the nail, not his. At least that's the best way he could reason it.

While he was trying to work out what the fuck had happened she booted him into the swamp. He couldn't blame her for that, he had just threatened to kill her. At the time he one hundred percent meant it, but that urge wasn't with him anymore. In fact, he didn't have the urge to harm anybody ever again, which while a new feeling for Swamp Boy, was a familiar feeling for the man before Swamp Boy.

He couldn't remember his name before he became Swamp Boy. Couldn't remember much of his previous life at all in fact, but he knew he wasn't born Swamp Boy. This was a suit put on him both in a literal sense, and a metaphorical one. Whoever he was before had no desire to ever hurt anyone, let alone kill like Swamp Boy had done many times.

He had sunk to the bottom of the swamp wondering what all this meant. This sudden release from his mental prison. Was it on purpose? Had he served his time for whatever crime he had committed? Or was it all by chance? Had he unknowingly been reset, his mind freed once again? Was this mind his own once more, could he think for himself? He hadn't been able to

214

think like this before he contemplated, in an early attempt to separate himself from Swamp Boy. He hadn't had any existential thoughts while under his spell. Although spell might not quite be the right word but he wasn't sure what was. Something to work out some other time.

Whilst lying at the bottom of the swamp he had become keenly aware, to a degree, he was in fact still kind of Swamp Boy. His physical appearance hadn't changed. His gills still allowed him to breathe underwater and he examined his webbed hands and feet noting they also hadn't changed. Would he change back to his old self, or was this it now? Was he now a man stuck in the body of a monster or were more changes afoot?

So far all he could tell was that only his mind was going through a change, and some of his own thoughts had returned. He did, however, still have more memories of being the monster than being himself. He just knew there was a self before there ever was a monster and that was a big revelation. A massive deal. He didn't start out as a monster, he had once been human. He checked his hands and feet again but they still remained the same, still webbed and slimy. He still had the same eyes and mouth too, he could feel it. He wanted his old body back, not that he was entirely sure what his old body looked like, but he had already grown impatient for its return. He was already worried it would never come back despite not knowing any of the rules of this world yet. He just felt that if his mind was returning, then his body should have started the process too.

Swamp Boy briefly considered staying in the abyss of the swamp forever if he was to remain in this monstrous state. He'd hurt a lot of people, killed almost as many, and he was struggling with these thought. He wasn't entirely sure why, but he knew he was a good guy before this and was eager to return to that. A good guy made to do terrible things his mind reasoned. While he had his free will back, he also had his conscious back, and the two were at loggerheads.

No, he couldn't stay in this darkness forever. What purpose would that serve? It was true he had committed unspeakable acts of terror and evil, but now he could do something about it. Now he could try to redeem himself if he was truly worthy. He may still look like Swamp Boy, but he wasn't that monster anymore. At least not where it truly counted. He was something else. Maybe not his normal self yet, but hopefully something heading in that direction.

He swam upwards from the depths of the swamp and burst its banks for the last time, and for the first time not to kill. He looked around and saw a pathway leading away from the swamp. It wasn't one he'd ever seen before but he wasn't sure if he'd ever really looked. Everything was still a mess in his head as the real him slowly began to regain territory within his mind. All the time spent as Swamp Boy hadn't left him. That was still there hanging over him, but it wasn't his centre anymore. None of the monster's nature was driving him. He really did have his free will back, and his free will told him to follow the path. And that path would lead him to Abby.

He had wronged this girl. Sure she'd fucking mercilessly killed him and kicked him to the bottom of the swamp as though he was nothing, but he had threatened her life when all she wanted to do was get out of this place. Maybe she was stuck here like him? Maybe she had answers he didn't and the pair could help each other - if she forgave him of course. He'd already forgiven her for killing him, although really he knew he should be thanking her for setting him free regardless of her intention.

Swamp Boy headed down the path once more thinking for himself. He hoped his memories would come back but for the moment he was glad he at least had his old instincts, his own intuition. It felt like a miracle that the monster no longer had a hold over him. He hoped this path would lead him where he needed to go, and something inside him was already telling him it would, and that he needed to hurry.

*

Swamp boy pulled Abby's limp body from the trough. He carefully lay her on the floor and wiped the blood from her face. Her eyes were closed and her mouth and nose showed no signs of breath. He carefully moved his webbed hands to her neck and checked for a pulse. His claws were retracted and he was being as gentle as he could which was no easy feat for some kind of fish monster creature with webbed clawed hands.

There was no pulse. Swamp Boy began CPR interlocking his webbed fingers the best he could and compressing them on her chest as gently as possible. He checked Abby's mouth for any leftover bloody water, and whatever other nasty shit was floating around in the trough, then continued. He gave her mouth to mouth wiping the blood from her lips first. He repeated the process again getting anxious at her lack of response until she spluttered back to life much to his, and probably Abby's, relief.

Abby coughed up a bucket of bloody water and took breaths of her own as it hit the floor. She was alive once more. Abby continued to take deep breaths in between being sick and gasping for the air to return to her lungs. She opened her eyes to see Swamp Boy keenly watching and hoping she was ok.

Abby sat upright looking at Swamp Boy as she wiped the drool from her mouth. She seemed aware he had saved her and wasn't an immediate threat. She'd had enough of those for one day already, including their own earlier encounter.

"You taste like blood and fish," she mumbled.

Swamp Boy laughed for what felt like the first time in ages.

His laugh was a normal human laugh rather than some kind of fish creature laugh.

"Thank you," she said in a sincere manner. For all her sarcasm and wit she knew when someone had done right by her, and Swamp Boy had saved her life.

He nodded to indicate it was no big deal but was also secretly pleased for himself. It felt like maybe his road to redemption had already begun. Obviously, he didn't want it to start in the manner it had, with Abby dead and needing to be brought back to life, but it had, and he had done the right thing.

But he had killed for the first time as himself too, or at least the first time with his own mind. He didn't know Psycho Hillbilly but knew everything about him was evil when he laid eyes on him. That was solidly backed up by him drowning Abby in a bath of blood. But still, he'd promised himself when he left the swamp not to kill again and then proceeded to violently push a man into vertical saws until no part of him was left. He'd barely gone an hour with that promise

He reasoned to himself that maybe a tiny bit of the monster was still inside him. Like it needed one last hurrah and best it should happen to some slasher killer rather than another innocent person. A need to get the poison out type thing. That was the last time, he strictly told himself like an addict who had relapsed but was determined to stay on the right path. Psycho Hillbilly was to be his last kill, because he was not a killer, far from it in fact. What he had done as Swamp Boy needed to be undone somehow and he'd take responsibility for his actions

"Psycho Hillbilly?" Abby asked, more for herself than sensing Swamp Boys' thoughts.

Swamp Boy looked to the vertical saw machine, then to the remains dripping from the barn roof. Abby nodded in satisfaction that he was dead, again, hopefully for keeps this time.

"Abby," she said holding her hand out to formally greet him.

Swamp Boy shook her hand but didn't have a name of his own to give back. She wanted to ask more than just his real name, had a hundred different questions including how was he still alive and why the fuck had he saved her, but then she remembered Whitney.

Abby was in no state to find her so sent Swamp Boy off to look instead. A trail of blood on the floor had led him to the meat locker when he got close. Opening the storage door he found her inside practically stuck to the icy floor. Like Abby, Whitney also wasn't breathing. Swamp Boy had to cut some of her hair with his claws to get her loose and carry her out of the freezer, but she'd later forgive him for that as she too was brought back to life when he warmed her up and performed CPR. It was quite a few minutes for a creature of the deep. If he was keeping score in his renewed life he'd killed one and saved two. As far as the beginnings of redeeming himself went it was a positive start despite the pushing a guy into saws incident.

Whitney looked up at him as she breathed and he knew she wasn't looking at an ugly fish creature from the swamp. He felt she really saw him as someone who had saved her. It had been a long time since he'd meet someone new who smiled at him rather than run in fear. It was a nice feeling and one he wanted to experience many more times, looking like a monster or not.

Swamp Boy carried Whitney over to Abby who was still on the floor trying to take everything that had happened in. She put her arms round Whitney when Swamp Boy placed her beside her. Whitney looked in an even worse state than Abby but the pair were both grateful to be alive and glad to see each other once more. They'd survived Psycho Hillbilly and he wasn't coming back this time. Whitney was finally free of him.

Both girls looked up at Swamp Boy as he stood away from them unsure what to say or do next.

"Didn't I kill you?" Abby finally bluntly asked breaking what was turning into an awkward silence.

"I think you brought me back to life," Swamp Boy replied with his voice again sounding more human and glad he could actually speak in his new state. He sounded closer to a kid in his twenties than a monster from the deep who just sort of gargled stuff.

"You're going to have to explain that one to me later," Abby said thinking that her brain couldn't handle any more today. She just wanted a shower and some clean clothes, not a long-winded explanation as to how Swamp Boy came back to life to save her, no matter how grateful she was for it.

"Thank you," Whitney offered with another smile, not needing the how's and why's, just pleased to be alive despite needing urgent medical attention, and a hairdresser.

Before she could add any more, or he could reply, a static buzzing interrupted the conversation. It sounded like feedback from a microphone, or more accurately, a microphone being switched on.

Percy's Rant

Percy stood beside the microphone table in the Splatploitation Brothers Studio's private cinema. The four of them had watched events unfold and cheered as Whitney had crawled to her death and shouted in delight as Psycho Hillbilly survived once more to come back and kill Abby. They laughed and chuckled as she desperately tried to escape his bloody drowning attempt knowing there was no fucking way in hell she could survive. Their latest scream queen was going to die a horrible, horrible death, the hallmark of any great Splatploitation Brothers movie, even if this one was more of a private homemade film just for their own viewing pleasure. But then they watched as that traitorous backstabbing Benedict Arnold motherfucker Swamp Boy turned his back on evil and saved the day by not only killing their creation Psycho Hillbilly, but also reviving those insolent girls. Naturally the air and enthusiasm had been sucked out of the room when Abby breathed life once more.

Matthew couldn't believe his beloved Psycho Hillbilly was dead. He was still hoping for Hillbilly Farm Two in the real world but knew Percy considered the Splatploitation World an extension of their films so there was no chance of that now considering there was nothing left of him. He quietly cursed Swamp Boy and vowed to get his revenge while doing his best not to cry in front of the others. Matthew could hold a grudge better than anyone, so in his eyes Swamp Boy's days were numbered. Abby wasn't off the hook though. For Matthew she was still public enemy number one for repeatedly trashing his acting and kicking him in the balls, which still hurt.

Roger shook his head disappointed at Swamp Boy too. He didn't mind the girls surviving, it just gave them more of a chance to torture and scare them, but he was upset that one of his creations had betrayed them. Swamp Boy was far from his favourite creature, but it was one of his creatures nonetheless so this felt a little embarrassing. Much like Matthew, he too swore revenge on Swamp Boy but for somewhat different reasons and in all honesty Roger didn't overly mean it. He'd forget about it soon enough. Matthew, however, would not.

Percy was not one to stand back and be happy with any of this either. This was not what he had in mind when he upgraded Psycho Hillbilly. Neither was it what he had in mind when he lead Abby to Hillbilly Farm. This was about as far from his vision as you could get and that included Swamp Boy's betrayal. It was almost too much, but Percy wasn't close to accepting defeat. No chance of live and let live, or the best person won, or any of that other hippy bullshit. As far as he was concerned he had been wronged. His artistic integrity had been put on the line and he was not going to allow that.

"This isn't how my films end, Goddammit!" he shouted to the room.

On the screen, Abby, Whitney, and Swamp Boy all looked somewhat confused while staring upwards at something. But only one person in the Splatploitation Brothers cinema had paid attention to their strange onscreen behaviour as Duncan curiously watched them. Roger and Matthew hadn't noticed anything as they were looking at Percy waiting for him to continue his explosion. Duncan however, watched Abby talking to Whitney on the screen as both looked directly upwards. He couldn't make out what was being said. The screen had been muted after they defeated Psycho Hillbilly with Percy in no mood to hear their annoying fucking gloating voices. Duncan's eyes drifted from the screen to the table beside Percy where he noticed exactly what was up.

Duncan began to speak but Percy instantly interrupted him

because he was a long way from being done and this needed to be said. This was the first time anything like this had happened and he would be damned if he wasn't going to address it. Sure, plenty happened in the Splatploitation World which was far from their control, but nothing like this. If they wanted someone they banished there dead, they mostly died. This was the first time the tables had been truly turned. Others had survived, but only because the Splatploitation Brothers decided to let them. Because they wanted further entertainment and amusement just like they'd repeatedly got from Whitney, or they'd forgotten about them. Not this time though. They wanted Abby dead and she had lived. That shouldn't have happened, that can't be. That's not how they do business.

If he had let Duncan speak however Percy would have been informed that he had leant backwards and switched the microphone on. Something which Duncan had noticed but no one else had. That particular microphone was a direct link to the onscreen Splatploitation World and therefore everything he was about to say would be heard by Abby, Whitney, and Swamp Boy. But as always he didn't let Duncan speak, and therefore didn't know that they were about to hear everything.

"Who does that girl think she is?" Percy continued. "What makes her so special? Victims do not survive in my films. In our films," he corrected but didn't completely mean it, he was the auteur after all. Roger and Matthew nodded in complete agreement while Duncan once again tried to inform Percy about the microphone but was shut down before he even got the first word out.

"They never make it to the end credits and neither will she. Or that fucking bimbo. Or that stupid fucking traitor fish who we should have canned years ago," he raged.

"She won't escape the Splatploitation World. We will punish her, torture her, ruin her, and scare every last witty remark out of her," Percy continued like a general on the battlefield motivating his troops for war. Roger and Matthew stood on his every word while Duncan's eyes were more on the screen watching the reaction of Abby and Co to Percy's rant.

"This is our world, our rules, and I'll be damned if some snooty little bitch and her dumb sidekick and ugly fish friend will fuck up my masterpiece," Percy continued looking for something to kick to further emphasise his rage. He didn't want to fuck up any of the equipment or the nice chairs though so he settled for throwing an empty soft drink can across the room.

"It's not my fault we put his costume on wrong," Roger intervened, unhappy at Percy's description of Swamp Boy. He could say it himself, he knew it was sub-par, but he didn't like it when others pointed out his less than stellar work. "I was in a rush," he added to his defence.

Percy stared at him not even sure what he was going on about until it occurred to him that he was talking about Swamp Boy's look and the fact that, as Abby had suspected, some of the costume had been put on incorrectly.

"I don't give a shit about that," Percy bluntly replied. "What I care about is them not getting to the end credits and escaping the Splatploitation World."

"The microphone is on," Duncan blurted out knowing he'd never get a chance to talk if he waited.

"The what?" Percy replied finally giving Duncan a little attention.

He turned to see the light on the microphone well and truly on meaning everything he just said had been heard in the Splatploitation World.

"The whole time?" Percy tentatively asked Duncan already knowing the answer.

Duncan nodded.

"Well why the fuck didn't you so say?" Percy blasted at him

as an argument interrupt in the room and the microphone got cut off.

*

Back in the Splatploitation World Abby, Whitney, and Swamp Boy had all stared upwards towards the part of the ceiling where Percy's voice had been booming down, as opposed to the part of the ceiling where Psycho Hillbilly's remains had been dripping down. Whitney was still holding the back of her head but a little more colour had come back to her in the course of overhearing the conversation. Abby too was looking a little better and breathing properly, again listening to Percy's words.

Swamp Boy looked the most confused of the three unsure what to make of the fact that half of him could possibly be on backwards. Sure, they'd just provided him with some information about how he got here, but he also felt embarrassed that the girls had heard how ridiculous he looks. Of course they both knew this already, having eyes and seeing him. In fact, Abby had already told him as much in their first encounter, but still, it hurt his pride a little hearing it even if he didn't want to be the monster anyway.

"Did he just monologue and tell us how to potentially escape this place?" Abby asked the other two breaking Swamp Boy's line of thought.

Both Whitney and Swamp Boy nonchalantly nodded almost in disbelief that any of that had just happened. The three looked at each other in united confusion for a moment before breaking into little smiles. They might not fully understand where they are, or how this world came to be, and they still didn't really know how they got here, or how exactly they could get out, but they did now know there was a way out. They knew it was possible to escape this place. That there was a chance.

Abby looked back towards the roof where the voice had come from with a grin on her face and a mocking tone in her voice.

"You guys really do suck."

The End.

ABBY,WHITNEY, AND SWAMP BOY WILL RETURN IN...

ABBY VS THE SPLATPLOITATION BROTHERS SAVAGE CITY

Printed in Great Britain
by Amazon

13176958R00132